AMERICANAH

Chimamanda Ngozi Adichie

*sparknotes

*spark notes

© 2020 SparkNotes LLC

This 2020 edition printed for SparkNotes LLC by Sterling Publishing Co., Inc.

ISBN 978-1-4114-8024-7

Distributed in Canada by Sterling Publishing Co., Inc.
c/o Canadian Manda Group, 664 Annette Street
Toronto, Ontario M6S 2C8, Canada
Distributed in the United Kingdom by GMC Distribution Services
Castle Place, 166 High Street, Lewes, East Sussex BN7 1XU, England
Distributed in Australia by NewSouth Books
University of New South Wales, Sydney, NSW 2052, Australia

For information about custom editions, special sales, and premium and corporate
purchases, please contact Sterling Special Sales at 800-805-5489
or specialsales@sterlingpublishing.com.

Manufactured in Canada

Lot #;
2 4 6 8 10 9 7 5 3 1
09/20

sparknotes.com
sterlingpublishing.com

Please email content@sparknotes.com to report any errors.

CONTENTS

C himamanda Ngozi Adichie was born on September 15, 1977, in Enugu, Nigeria, and grew up in Nsukka, where the University of Nigeria is located. Her parents worked for the university, her father as a professor and her mother as the first female registrar of the university. Her family is Igbo, one of the three major ethnic groups of Nigeria, along with the Yoruba and Hausa. Although she began studying medicine at the University of Nigeria, Adichie longed to study the humanities and later received a scholarship to Drexel University in Philadelphia, which changed her course of study. After two years, she transferred to Eastern Connecticut University, where she graduated summa cum laude with a BA in political science and communications. She then attended Johns Hopkins University for her MFA in creative writing and later received an MA in African studies from Yale University. Since then she has won numerous fellowships and awards, including a MacArthur Genius Grant in 2008. She now teaches in Nigeria and the United States.

Adichie's first novel, *Purple Hibiscus*, was published in 2003, and won the Commonwealth Writers' Prize for Best First Book in 2005. Following that, she wrote two novels, *Half of a Yellow Sun* and *Americanah*, plus numerous essays and short stories. In addition to her fiction, Adichie is well known as a speaker and essayist. Her two extremely popular TED Talks highlight themes that she explores throughout her creative work and quite clearly in *Americanah*. At 2009's TED Global Conference she presented "The Danger of a Single Story," which discusses the consequences of stereotypes in both fiction and reality. Her 2012 TED Talk, "We Should All Be Feminists," addressed the importance of raising both daughters and sons to create a fairer world. It has been downloaded millions of times and republished in book form. In 2013, Beyoncé sampled the talk on her song "***Flawless," bringing Adichie's message to the wider public.

Adichie worked on *Americanah* throughout 2011–2012, while on fellowship at the Radcliffe Institute for Advanced Study at Harvard University. The novel draws inspiration partially from her experiences in the United States throughout college and partially based on the experiences of friends. Like her character Ifemelu, Adichie was taken aback at being considered black in the United States and the negativity associated with the label. The book was released in

2013 to great reviews, winning the 2013 National Book Critics Circle Fiction Award. The *New York Times* listed it as one of the best ten books of the year, and it was chosen for the New York Public Library's 2017 "One Book, One New York" campaign. In 2018, actress Lupita Nyong'o announced that she was working to adapt the novel as a television miniseries. Former president Barack Obama included *Americanah* on his list of books by "a number of Africa's best writers and thinkers," a collection he compiled in 2018 in preparation for his first visits to Kenya and South Africa since his time in office. On that list, *Americanah* joins Chinua Achebe's *Things Fall Apart*, one of the undisputed classics of Nigerian literature.

After Nigeria's independence from the British Empire in 1960, the country faced a series of military coups, and the government passed from one general to another. The resulting instability had catastrophic effects on the nation's infrastructure. Poor working conditions and late payments for the staff of the universities caused strikes, and universities closed for months at a time. Amid this chaos, many Nigerians chose to immigrate to countries like the United States and Britain in search of opportunities. Adichie has said that she wanted to depict this kind of immigration in *Americanah*, one of middle-class immigrants on a quest for opportunity, rather than fleeing danger. In 1998, the then head of state, General Abubakar, brought forward a new plan to return Nigeria's power to an elected president. The 1999 elections proceeded as planned, bringing Olusegun Obasanjo to power. However, corruption and conflict still plagued the country.

Ifemelu and Obinze's differing immigration experiences relate to the changes in the United States and Britain after the terrorist attacks of September 11, 2001. Among other new security measures, the United States created a new Department of Homeland Security, which took over the scrutiny of visa applications, leading to more rejections overall. Similar immigrant paranoia reached Britain, and the home secretary at the time, David Blunkett, worked toward stricter immigration laws and even proposed implementing identification cards for British citizens. These fears and bureaucratic difficulties added to the already challenging immigration landscapes of these countries. Also important to the novel are Ifemelu's frank and often humorous observations of race in America. These experiences become tied to the nomination and eventual election of Barack Obama as the first black president of the United States in 2008. His central campaign messages of hope and change resonated both as an alternative to the fear that typified previous administrations and as the dream that the United States was ready for a black president despite its deep racial divide.

PLOT OVERVIEW

Ifemelu, a Nigerian woman who lives in Princeton, New Jersey, gets her hair braided in preparation for her upcoming return to Nigeria. She has broken up with her boyfriend, Blaine, closed her popular blog about race, and uprooted her life because she feels weighed down. When she thinks of returning to Nigeria, she can't help but think of Obinze, her first love, now a wealthy man in Lagos with a wife and daughter. Upon receiving an email from Ifemelu, Obinze becomes distracted. He has stumbled into wealth after his cousin introduces him to a well-connected man. His wife, Kosi, is beautiful and adoring, but they never connected on the emotional level that he and Ifemelu did. That night, he listens to the music he and Ifemelu used to listen to when they made love.

The novel flashes back to Ifemelu's youth. She and Obinze meet at a party where a friend attempts to set Obinze up with a girl named Ginika. Obinze has admired Ifemelu from afar since transferring to their school, and they immediately hit it off. They date all throughout secondary school and through the start of college. However, university lecturer strikes keep closing the universities, and Obinze and Aunty Uju encourage Ifemelu to apply to school in America. Ifemelu is accepted and then quickly approved for a student visa. Ifemelu and Obinze plan to one day reunite in America. Unfortunately, Ifemelu's student visa does not allow her to work, and without a full scholarship and stipend, Ifemelu must find a source of income. She applies for jobs using a family friend's social security card, to no avail. In desperation, she agrees to work for a shady tennis coach as his "relaxation assistant," which involves allowing him to touch her sexually. After one meeting, she never returns to the coach. Out of shame and self-loathing, she stops replying to Obinze's messages and emails.

Ifemelu succeeds when Ginika introduces her to Kimberly, a white woman who needs a babysitter. The steady work offers her a chance to focus on her studies. She meets Kimberly's wealthy cousin, Curt, who is immediately smitten with her. They start dating, and when Ifemelu graduates, Curt helps her get a job that will sponsor her green card. For the job interview, Ifemelu decides to have her hair relaxed so that it will look professional according to American standards. The relaxer burns her scalp, and her friend Wambui encourages her to try wearing her hair natural. At first, Ifemelu thinks her hair is ugly, but soon grows to love it. One day, she runs into a friend from Nigeria who asks what happened between her and Obinze. She gives him the cold shoulder and is upset the rest of the day. Although she explains that the university friend was not an ex-boyfriend, Curt acts possessive.

Meanwhile, Obinze lives as an illegal immigrant in London. His American visa application was rejected because of anti-terror panic after the September 11 attacks. His mother offers to bring him as a research assistant on a trip to London as a way to get him into Britain. Obinze's friend links him up with a fellow Nigerian, Vincent, who is willing to let him use his national insurance card in order to work if Obinze will give him a percentage of his income. Obinze agrees and finds a job in a warehouse. Eventually, Vincent demands more money. Obinze refuses, and the next day his boss tells him that someone reported him as an illegal immigrant. Desperate, Obinze tries to find someone to arrange a green card marriage for him. The day Obinze's wedding is meant to take place, he arrives at the courthouse only to find the police awaiting him. Obinze is deported.

Ifemelu cheats on Curt and ends their relationship. After she writes an email to Wambui detailing her frustration with Curt's inability to understand the necessity of *Essence* magazine in a world of beauty magazines catering to white women, Wambui suggests Ifemelu start blogging. Ifemelu starts a blog focusing on her observations on race in America as a non-American black woman, and her clever posts soon lead to its popularity. At a conference for minority bloggers, she runs into Blaine, a black American professor at Yale. They begin dating, and Ifemelu moves in with him. When Ifemelu does not attend a protest Blaine organizes against the university's racial profiling of a black staff member, they have a major fight and almost break up. However, Barack Obama's presidential candidacy draws them back together and gives them a joint mission up until the election and Ifemelu's subsequent decision to leave.

Aunty Uju calls Ifemelu to tell her that her son, Dike, tried to kill himself. Ifemelu rushes to be with him. Once back in Nigeria, Ifemelu slowly finds her feet. However, she is hesitant to contact Obinze. Finally, she texts him, and he wants to meet up with her as soon as possible. Their attraction is still undeniable. When Obinze asks her why she cut him off, Ifemelu tells him the story of the tennis coach, surprised at her own tears. Obinze holds her hand, and she basks in the safety she feels. After more dates, Ifemelu awkwardly rekindles their sexual relationship, although she does not want to be his mistress. They argue, and Ifemelu calls Obinze a coward for not divorcing Kosi. Shaken, Obinze thinks about Ifemelu's accusation and finds truth in it. He asks Kosi for a divorce. Kosi tries to ignore his declaration, reminding him that he has a duty to his family. Obinze decides that he doesn't want his daughter to grow up with her parents only playing the roles of happy husband and wife. Days later, he shows up at Ifemelu's flat telling her that he has left Kosi, will continue to be present in his daughter's life, and wants to be with Ifemelu. Ifemelu invites him in.

Character List

Ifemelu   The titular Americanah and protagonist of the novel, a Nigerian woman who moves to America. Ifemelu is opinionated and disarmingly frank, to the point that it gets her into trouble. Despite her stubbornness, Ifemelu's journey to America is more an idea other people had for her than her own. Throughout the novel, she turns more to the markers of her true self, including her real accent, her natural hair, and eventually a return to Nigeria.

Obinze   Ifemelu's first love, a calm, thoughtful Nigerian man. Throughout the novel, Obinze is attracted to authenticity and he finds Ifemelu's honesty and bluntness refreshing. As a youth, Obinze loves the idea of America and believes it to be the future. After seeing the obstacles Nigerians must go through to succeed in America and Britain, he resolves to stay in Nigeria. Obinze becomes wealthy and falls into a superficial marriage with Kosi, but never falls out of love with Ifemelu.

Dike   The son of Aunty Uju and The General. Over the course of the novel, Dike grows from a bright and cheerful child to a confused and depressed teenager. He finds himself trapped between his peers' treatment of him as a black American and his mother's insistence that he is not a black American.

Aunty Uju   Ifemelu's aunt, a doctor who immigrates to America with her son, Dike. As a young woman in Nigeria, she offers practical advice to Ifemelu about growing up, but the pressures of rebuilding her life in America dampen Aunty Uju's spirit. Her willingness to allow others to control her destiny means Ifemelu, though younger, often is the one to emotionally support Aunty Uju.

Curt   Kimberly's cousin, a wealthy white man full of energy and optimism who dates Ifemelu. He enjoys giving Ifemelu lavish gifts and taking her to exotic destinations, even making sure she is able to find employment after graduation. However, Curt is also possessive of Ifemelu and unable to fully understand her.

Blaine An earnest and justice-minded black American man and a professor of political science. Blaine's strong principles often lead to conflict in his dating relationship with Ifemelu.

Ginika Ifemelu's beautiful and kind friend from secondary school, a popular girl whom Kayode wants to set up with Obinze. She is always voted the most beautiful girl in school, which she attributes to her mixed-race heritage. Ginika moves to America in her teens and later guides Ifemelu through her early days in America.

Ifemelu's father A thoughtful and proud man who attempts to mask his limited education with his large vocabulary. After he loses his job, he falls into a deep depression that plunges the family into dire financial straits.

Ifemelu's mother A religious woman who tries to smooth over difficulties with her extreme faith.

Obinze's mother An intelligent and practical professor. She is earnest and frank about difficult topics, such as sex, preferring honesty except when forced to lie for her son.

Kosi Obinze's wife, a beautiful and bubbly Nigerian woman. Kosi wants her life with Obinze to remain smooth and seamless, and she can be counted on to charm her way through any difficult social situation. The value she places on appearance over honesty makes her a foil for Ifemelu.

Shan Blaine's dazzling older sister. Shan has a magnetic personality that she uses to host parties featuring artists and intellectuals she admires; however, she expects to remain at the center of these gatherings and is often very selfish.

Kimberly   A good-hearted but privileged white woman who offers Ifemelu a babysitting job in America. Kimberly's "white guilt" causes her to apologize constantly, which initially makes it difficult for Ifemelu to befriend her.

Wambui   Ifemelu's friend from college, a Kenyan woman studying in Philadelphia on a student visa. Wambui takes Ifemelu to her first meeting of the African Students Union, allowing Ifemelu to connect with other African students at the university, and she later encourages Ifemelu to embrace the style of natural hair.

Chief   An extremely wealthy Nigerian man whom Obinze curries favor with in hopes of finding a job in Lagos.

The General   An important man in the military government of Nigeria who is having an affair with Aunty Uju. He is extremely controlling and arranges Aunty Uju's life so she depends completely upon him. He is also Dike's father.

Nicholas   Obinze's cousin who has moved to London. Although his university years were spent rebelling, in London he is now serious and stolid, with no trace of his former energy.

Ojiugo   Nicholas's wife. In Nigeria, she was as rebellious as Nicholas, but in London she devotes all her energy to playing the role of dutiful wife and mother, projecting all her dreams onto her children.

Nigel   Obinze's coworker at the London warehouse, a young and insecure man who befriends Obinze and always splits their tips evenly.

Roy   Obinze's warm and cheerful boss at the London warehouse.

Doris   Ifemelu's coworker at *Zoe*, a young, obsequious woman determined to remain in Aunty Onenu's good graces. She has recently returned to Nigeria from America and constantly reminds everyone of this fact.

Laura Kimberly's sister, a demanding and bitter white woman. She meddles in Kimberly's life, even discouraging her from hiring Ifemelu.

Boubacar A Senegalese immigrant, a pretentious but kind professor at Yale who encourages Ifemelu to apply for the Princeton fellowship.

Zemaye Ifemelu's coworker at *Zoe*, a prickly but intelligent young woman with no patience for Doris's airs.

Aunty Onenu Ifemelu's boss at *Zoe*, a society woman more interested in defeating her rival in women's magazine publishing than running a business.

Aisha The African woman braiding Ifemelu's hair throughout the novel. She annoys Ifemelu with her constant questions, but these hide her desperation to obtain American citizenship.

Paula Blaine's ex-girlfriend, a white woman and fellow academic. Her zeal for social justice matches Blaine's and reminds Ifemelu that there is a bond they share that she will never understand.

Kayode The most popular student at Ifemelu's secondary school. He wants to set Obinze up with Ginika.

Bartholomew Aunty Uju's American husband, a selfish man who expects to use Aunty Uju for money and housekeeping.

Vincent Obi A Nigerian immigrant in Britain, a greedy swindler who extorts money from Obinze by lending him his insurance card.

Ranyinudo One of Ifemelu's Nigerian friends who helps Ifemelu reacquaint herself to life in Lagos.

Cristina Tomas The rude receptionist at the registrar's office at Wellson. Ifemelu adopts an American accent after Cristina assumes Ifemelu has only a tenuous grasp of English.

Esther   The receptionist at *Zoe*, a naïve and superstitious woman who believes her church's prosperity doctrine will bring her fortune.

Emenike   A friend of Obinze's from university who becomes patronizing upon growing his wealth.

Georgina   Emenike's wife, an intelligent British lawyer.

Cleotilde   Obinze's fiancée for his green card marriage.

Buchi   Obinze and Kosi's daughter.

Morgan   Kimberly's surly daughter.

ANALYSIS OF MAJOR CHARACTERS

IFEMELU

Although the novel switches between Ifemelu's and Obinze's perspectives, Ifemelu is the protagonist of *Americanah* because her self-actualization lies at the narrative's heart. Ifemelu's departure for America ignites the major conflict: her separation from Obinze. Despite Ifemelu's independent spirit, she doesn't initiate her immigration to America, but agrees to Obinze's American dream in part because of Obinze's belief that America is the future. In America, Ifemelu struggles as she's labeled "black" for the first time in her life and discovers the racism prevalent, if not overt, in American society. As the novel progresses, Ifemelu becomes more comfortable rejecting American culture and white standards of beauty in favor of her authentic Nigerian self. She drops her American accent and wears her hair in its natural texture because she wants to be her true self. Her blog makes her feel fake because she must strain to understand race in America as an outsider. Therefore, her return to Nigeria is a return to her authentic self, the person she can be effortlessly. At the very end of the novel, while Ifemelu is sad at the possibility of losing Obinze, she is fully prepared to live without him because she has achieved a more complete sense of self by embracing her Nigerian identity.

OBINZE

Obinze is primarily characterized by his desire for truth and authenticity. While others fear Ifemelu's blunt honesty, he finds it attractive, more so than the niceness promised by Ginika. Later, in his marriage, he tries to provoke Kosi into honesty by telling her blatant lies, attempting to make her more like Ifemelu, who is never afraid to disagree with him. After he is deported from England, he reflects that he will not try to immigrate again because he possesses enough relative privilege that, for him, truth does not have to be a "luxury." For poorer immigrants, the financial opportunities available in England are such a drastic improvement over their lives in Nigeria that they prefer the deceit necessitated by illegal immigration. Obinze, however, grew up solidly middle class. He can afford to live honestly in Nigeria and does not judge all the lying he had to go through—a fake ID card, an attempted green card marriage—to have been worth his hardships. At the end of the novel, part of his motivation for leaving Kosi is to not subject Buchi to watching her parents live a lie, again choosing a difficult truth over a pleasing fiction.

DIKE

Dike demonstrates the importance of embracing one's history. Dike grows up without roots because his mother, Aunty Uju, refuses to tell him the truth about his father and cuts him off from a Nigerian identity. This rootlessness leads to confusion because of the identities other people project onto him. Because of the negative associations of blackness in America, Aunty Uju constantly tells Dike that he is not black, but because white Americans hold the same racist stereotypes for everyone with black skin, Dike still must carry the baggage. Later, he uses African-American Vernacular English (AAVE) in order to conform to others' expectations of what it means to be black. Ifemelu blames this confusion for his suicide attempt, that Aunty Uju has told Dike who he is not, but not who he is. Dike's visit to Nigeria, therefore, offers him a chance to heal. After Ifemelu shows him the house he spent his infancy in, he asks if he can drive them home. Here, Dike takes the wheel and implies that he has control over his identity again. Other people can no longer determine his identity for him because he now understands where he came from.

AUNTY UJU

Aunty Uju begins the novel as Ifemelu's mentor but shifts to a cautionary figure due to her willingness to subjugate herself for the promise of comfort. She justifies her dependence on The General by claiming that success in Nigeria relies on kissing up to powerful people. To maintain this success, she undergoes costly beauty treatments and devotes her time to false friendships, valuing The General's standards over her own. However, this success proves to be fragile because she must uproot her life after The General dies. Her willingness to submit to power for immediate gain also reveals itself in her new, subdued personality in America. Ifemelu notices that Aunty Uju tries to Americanize herself quickly to gain acceptance. Aunty Uju can't even laugh with Ifemelu about Americanisms because to laugh at them would be to deny their power to make her successful. Her initial interest in Bartholomew seems to be a desire to replicate her life with The General, and she leaves once she realizes that he will not bring her success. Aunty Uju's constant sublimation of self contrasts with Ifemelu's journey of self-honesty.

Themes, Motifs & Symbols

Themes

Themes are the fundamental and often universal ideas explored in a literary work.

The Importance of Authenticity

The characters in *Americanah* suffer when forced to deny their true selves and emotions but find joy in the authentic, positing that honesty is the key to a happy life. Even unpleasant truths become worse when not told, as when Aunty Uju's refusal to tell Dike about The General leads Dike to assume that he was unloved by his father. The falsehoods involved in immigration, from affecting an accent to using false identification, cause emotional strain and lead to feelings of inferiority and invisibility. Ifemelu delights in a piece of junk mail addressed to her because it has her name on it and is proof that she exists even as she attempts to find jobs as someone else. Above all, we see this appreciation of and desire for honesty in Ifemelu and Obinze's relationship. Obinze's love of Ifemelu's bluntness causes her to find value in herself just as she is, and she chases this feeling of rightness and ease throughout the novel. Obinze recognizes the strain his divorce causes both Kosi and Buchi, but explicitly says that he doesn't want Buchi to grow up in a lie, emphasizing again that embracing uncomfortable truths—not hiding them—is the key to long-term happiness.

Race and Racism

Ifemelu quickly discovers that in America, white Americans treat her as a black American, despite the fact that she's from Africa. Throughout the novel, this confusing conflation of blackness creates tension for Adichie's characters. Characters like Aunty Uju attempt to distance themselves from black Americans because, as Ifemelu notes, black Americans have the least amount of privilege in the American racial hierarchy. This distancing fails because white Americans in the novel do not differentiate by culture, and Aunty Uju faces discrimination. Ifemelu notices that white Americans pit all black people against each other despite their extremely different histories, such as when Laura speaks of her Ugandan classmate who didn't get along with the black American woman in her class. Furthermore, the singular category of "black" leads black Americans in *Americanah* to assume that black non-Americans have an intrinsic understanding of their struggles. For example, Ifemelu disappoints Blaine for not caring as deeply as he does about the discrimination against Mr. White. While she can notice the horrific treatment of black Americans, this treatment will never be personal to Ifemelu. She feels that the American categorization of race flattens disparate peoples, conflating groups that don't necessarily understand each other.

MOTIFS

Motifs are recurring structures, contrasts, or literary devices that can help to develop and inform the text's major themes.

READING AND NOVELS

Throughout *Americanah*, novels say as much about the people who read them as the subjects they cover, and characters' taste in novels offers glimpses into their personalities. After her breakup with Blaine, Ifemelu intentionally reads a book that Blaine dismissed as trivial, because she assumes she will like it. Obinze laments his inability to love Graham Greene's *The Heart of the Matter*, hoping that understanding it would bring him closer to his mother. Furthermore, characters assign depth to people who love books. Carrying a novel makes Ifemelu instantly interesting to Obinze. However, when The General brags that Aunty Uju requests books as a present, his misogynistic assumption that this is a rare female trait reveals he does not expect intelligence from women. Similarly, Obinze's request for a book while in holding shocks the police out of the incorrect assumption that illegal immigrants would not be interested in an intellectual pastime. In this way, reading becomes shorthand for having a vibrant and curious inner life, and the assumptions of The General and the immigration officials reveal their bigoted understandings of who is capable of cultivating this kind of inner life.

LIES

Over the course of the novel, characters lie and deceive as a survival mechanism. Ifemelu and Obinze must pretend to be other people in order to make the money they need to survive in a new country. Ifemelu has a habit of exaggerating how long she's lived in America so that people take her comments seriously, meaning that she must lie in order for her voice to be heard. The necessity of these lies demonstrates that in the corrupt, complicated world of immigration, dishonesty may not be ideal but it is a means of survival. However, Ifemelu's return to Nigeria involves her embracing truth. She refuses to live duplicitously in her relationship with Obinze and won't allow him to explain away their dates as not truly being an affair. This change emphasizes the hopeful tone of the ending, one in which Ifemelu embraces her Nigerian self and is able to survive honestly.

SYMBOLS

> *Symbols are objects, characters, figures, or colors used to represent abstract ideas or concepts.*

BARACK OBAMA

Ifemelu, Blaine, and Blaine's friends all see Obama as a symbol of hope for the future of America. However, despite Ifemelu's observation that everyone in their group seems to agree on Obama, they do not actually agree on what specific hopes Obama represents. Obama's multifaceted family history allows for multiple interpretations of what his election to office means. He is the child of a poor Kenyan father, and therefore his success seems to comment on the possibility of the American dream for someone like Dike. Black Americans also see him as representative of progress. Ifemelu's blog posts highlight the myriad meanings projected onto Obama, including the possibility of black men seeing beauty in black women and a magical black man who will soothe white anxiety about racism. The way in which Obama and his presidential candidacy represent so many hopes at the same time, therefore, symbolizes the complex and often contradictory nature of the racial category of "black" as it exists in America.

HAIR

Ifemelu reclaiming her natural hair mirrors her accepting of her Nigerian identity. When she first cuts her hair, Ifemelu believes her hair to be ugly. This shame is similar to how she's made to feel about her Nigerian accent, leading her to affect an American one. Just as she considers her American accent to be a false air she puts on, by relaxing her hair she forces a part of herself to contort into an unnatural shape. Others do not allow Ifemelu's hair to be a neutral representation of Ifemelu's identity. Ifemelu's coworkers assume her hair is a political statement. Her Nigerian friends don't understand her natural hairstyle, mirroring how Nigerian immigrants throughout the novel find Western culture alluring. Although caring for her natural hair takes effort, Ifemelu finds joy in conditioning, contrasted against the stress of relaxing her hair. Similarly, her return to Nigeria has challenges, but she finds satisfaction instead of doubt in writing about Lagos. Ifemelu's love of her hair, therefore, matches her love of Nigeria, and she finds joy in authenticity.

THE MALE PEACOCK

Ifemelu's desire to see the male peacock dance culminates in an anticlimax where the female peacock rejects his advances, highlighting the ultimate failure of superficial splendor. Ifemelu has just returned from America, which, despite its glossy promise of success, has only led her to return to the more chaotic Lagos, which she feels is authentic to her identity. Like the glossy images of America, the male peacock is beautiful, but his beauty does not seduce the female peacock. The failure of the male peacock also echoes Obinze's failed attempt to carry on an affair with Ifemelu. Although Obinze has shown Ifemelu his new wealth and even implied a willingness to invest in her new blog, she finds it to be no substitute for living with him honestly. Like the male peacock, his lavish display of wealth does not hold up and results in Obinze looking as "ridiculous" as the bird itself. Ifemelu's growth throughout the novel is centered around embracing authenticity, and the female peacock's rejection of the male succinctly summarizes her newfound self, who prefers reality to a beautiful image.

Summary & Analysis

Part 1: Chapters 1–2

Summary: Chapter 1

Ifemelu, a young Nigerian woman living in America, awaits the train from Princeton to Trenton, New Jersey, to get her hair braided. Because Princeton is a primarily white city, there are no hair braiding salons. A man on the platform comments on the lateness of the train, and Ifemelu considers that there was a time where she would have told him about her blog on race in America or attempted to interview him. She recently closed her blog because she is moving back to Nigeria. She thinks about how all the commenters on her blog made her less sure of what she thought she knew, and the effort to find new post ideas makes her feel "naked and false."

When she leaves the train at Trenton, she notes that the passengers here are fatter than those at Princeton. She only recently started thinking of people as fat again because her friend told her that "fat" is an insult in America. However, after a man at a grocery insulted her, she realized that not only had she gained weight but also felt weighed down in her life, and she decided to return to Nigeria. She also cannot stop thinking about Obinze, her first love, and the only person she has ever felt she could be her whole self with. He lives in Lagos and now has a wife and a daughter. Ifemelu had a difficult time breaking up with her boyfriend Blaine and telling him she is returning to Nigeria. She does not have a good explanation and cannot tell him that she has always felt unsettled in their relationship.

Ifemelu goes to the salon, run by African immigrants, and a Senegalese woman named Aisha braids her hair. Aisha complains that Ifemelu does not relax her hair. Aisha is surprised to learn that Ifemelu is Igbo. Aisha is dating two Igbo men and would like to marry one of them. She asks whether Igbo people only marry other Igbo. Ifemelu disputes this. Ifemelu hastily sends Obinze an email while trying to ignore Aisha.

The women in the shop are impressed when they hear Ifemelu lives in Princeton and shocked to hear that she plans to return to Nigeria, asking whether she will be able to cope after being in America for so long. They ask if she has a man waiting for her. Ifemelu lies and says yes. Aisha insists that she will call her Igbo men so that Ifemelu can tell them Igbo do not have to marry other Igbo. Ifemelu thinks that if she still ran her blog, this would make a great blog post on how immigrant pressure makes people crazy.

SUMMARY: CHAPTER 2

Obinze stares at the email from Ifemelu. She has called him Ceiling, her old nickname for him. He wonders jealously about Ifemelu's black American boyfriend. Obinze's wife, Kosi, calls to ask where he is, and Obinze thinks about how she always tells him where she is during these calls even though he never asks her location.

He returns home. His house is full of expensive things, like imported Italian furniture and air conditioning. They have a housegirl from Benin because Kosi felt Nigerian housegirls were not suitable. Beautiful Kosi, who often gets mistaken for someone of mixed-race descent, greets him, along with their two-year-old daughter, Buchi. Obinze lies to Kosi about the status of the block of flats he is selling. He often tells her useless lies to see if she will challenge them, but she cares more about the consistency of their domestic life.

Obinze gets ready to go to Chief's party, dressing in the clothing Kosi has laid out for him. When Obinze returned to Nigeria from England, his cousin Nneoma introduced him to Chief, an extremely wealthy businessman. Chief had a crush on Nneoma, who constantly flattered him but refused to sleep with him. Thanks to Nneoma's ingratiation, Chief offered Obinze a job as a real estate evaluation consultant, which led to Obinze making a fortune.

At Chief's party, two guests debate the merits of Kosi sending Buchi to the French- or British-style schools, and Obinze, annoyed, observes that they all grew up with a Nigerian curriculum. The other guests are shocked that Obinze would suggest Nigerian schooling, but Kosi smooths over the conversation.

On the way home, Obinze thinks about how marriage changed Kosi into a jealous woman. The church she attends includes a prayer for keeping one's husband, and she fears single women. Before bed, he listens to Fela, a musical artist he and Ifemelu used to listen to when they slept together and composes another email to her.

ANALYSIS: CHAPTERS 1–2

As the novel begins, Ifemelu and Obinze's lives are mired in dishonesty, and these falsehoods have led to their dissatisfaction in life. While Ifemelu enjoys her blogging, she mentions that constantly searching for new topics for her posts makes her question her own judgment and the validity of her work. The effort it takes for her to create her posts leaves Ifemelu feeling like a fraud. In its current form, Ifemelu's blog is an explicitly American endeavor because it analyzes race in America. We can read some of her dissatisfaction with her American life, therefore, as a result of the effort she must make to live it, straining until she verges on lying. Obinze spends the entirety of Chapter 2 lamenting the falsehoods in his life, especially in regard to his wife, Kosi. Kosi makes a point never to reveal her true feelings on a subject, praising both sides of an argument in order to please everyone. Kosi's social ease causes Obinze's guilt about his true feelings and constant desire to disrupt order, such as when he challenges the idea that proper schooling in Nigeria is rooted in foreign curricula. Both Ifemelu and Obinze strain under the pressure to be people they're not.

These beginning chapters also establish that Ifemelu and Obinze see each other as sincere and authentic, which means that in their longing for each other, they also long for honesty. When Ifemelu thinks of Obinze, she describes him as the only person with whom she can be herself without explanation. This comfort contrasts with her interactions with other characters. For example, Aisha wants to know why Ifemelu does not relax her hair, condemning Ifemelu for allowing her hair to grow out naturally, and Ifemelu feels frustrated by Aisha's pressure. While Obinze's longing for Ifemelu appears rooted in his sexual attraction, he also emphasizes loving her honesty. He even tries to bait Kosi into acting more like Ifemelu by telling her obvious lies, but Kosi's desire to keep things peaceful leads her to ignore them. Ifemelu and Obinze have an attraction and connection rooted in embracing reality and truth.

These chapters also introduce the idea that Nigerians and other Africans associate leaving Nigeria (and Africa) with wealth and success. The hair braiders are shocked that Ifemelu, who lives in the wealthy American suburb Princeton, would wish to return to Nigeria, highlighting that they do not expect someone who has found success in America to return to her homeland. They imagine return as a step backward from progress, even suggesting that Ifemelu will no longer be able to cope with the realities of living in Nigeria again. Obinze's chapter echoes this devaluation of Nigeria. The imported Italian furniture and wife who looks biracial are part of what marks Obinze's life as successful to other Nigerians. Even sending Buchi to a school that does not promise a foreign curriculum is unthinkable for their social class, because they believe Nigerian education to be inferior. To the Nigerian characters in *Americanah*, success means distancing oneself from being Nigerian.

Despite Obinze's dismissal of Kosi's jealousy as a sign of her shallow conformity, Obinze's own actions suggest that Kosi has reason to worry about their marriage. From the moment Obinze hears that Ifemelu plans to return to Nigeria, he remembers their sexual encounters, not with nostalgia but with longing, even playing the music they made love to. He demonstrates that his feelings for Ifemelu remain alive by thinking with jealousy about her current boyfriend, despite being married himself. Obinze also demonstrates a lack of concern for Kosi by never checking on where she is, even though she always asks where he is. Kosi always volunteers this information, implying that she would perhaps like Obinze to take equal interest in her life.

PART 1: CHAPTERS 3–5

SUMMARY: CHAPTER 3

Chapter 3 begins a flashback to Ifemelu's childhood. Ifemelu's mother starts attending Guiding Assembly, a Christian church that preaches prosperity as its major doctrine, and passes the collection plate around three times per service. Her mother prays constantly for the safety of The General, an important statesman who has taken Ifemelu's Aunty Uju as a mistress. Ifemelu's mother calls him Aunty Uju's mentor, pointedly ignoring the sexual aspect of their relationship.

Meanwhile, Ifemelu's father loses his job. He tries to find a new job, but eventually gives up and mopes at home, forgetting even to shower at times. Ifemelu's mother blames this change in fortune on the devil. Ifemelu's father speaks with a British accent and uses large words as if to make up for never being able to get the kind of education he always longed for. As Ifemelu's father remains unemployed, eventually the family falls behind in their rent.

On the day Ifemelu is to go to see Aunty Uju's new estate gifted to her by The General, she gets in trouble with a powerful woman at church because she refuses to help make paper garlands for Chief Omenka, calling him a thief. The church woman accuses Ifemelu of being unwilling to do God's work. Ifemelu believes that both this woman and her mother use religion as a way of not seeing things as they really are.

After Ifemelu's father reminds Ifemelu that her tendency to go against authority has sullied her school record, Ifemelu's mother demands that Aunty Uju tell Ifemelu to behave. Aunty Uju has long acted as a big sister in Ifemelu's life, giving her sensible advice as she navigated puberty. After the incident at church, Aunty Uju again offers Ifemelu sisterly advice, reminding her that she does not always have to say her every thought.

Summary: Chapter 4

She rested her head against his and felt, for the first time, what she would often feel with him: a self-affection. He made her like herself. With him, she was at ease; her skin felt as though it was her right size.

(See QUOTATIONS, p. 65)

When Obinze joins Ifemelu's secondary school, rumors abound that he moved there because his mother fought with another professor at the university in Nsukka. This makes him instantly popular. Everyone expects him to go out with Ifemelu's friend Ginika. Ginika is sweet and always gets voted the prettiest girl in their class, but she claims it is only because she is half-caste and has a white mother. Kayode, the coolest boy in school, promises to introduce Obinze to Ginika at his upcoming party.

At the party, Obinze has a difficult time speaking to Ginika. Ifemelu blurts out a rude question about him wearing a jacket in the heat, which amuses him. Obinze and Ifemelu end up dancing and talking the whole night. Obinze tells her that he's admired her from afar because he saw her carrying a novel. He also liked that she had a reputation for being argumentative. Ifemelu points out that he's supposed to be after Ginika, and he replies, "I'm chasing you." Ifemelu appreciates his honesty and the way he makes her feel like herself. They kiss. From that moment on, they are an inseparable couple.

Summary: Chapter 5

Ginika's family immigrates to America, which goes smoothly because Ginika already has an American passport. The other students think having an American passport is cool. Ifemelu feels out of place because her poorer family doesn't have access to these foreign dreams. She worries that one day Obinze will tire of her bluntness and realize that a girl like Ginika, with access to America, is better suited to him.

Obinze's mother invites Ifemelu to lunch at their home. Obinze's mother looks like the Nigerian singer Onyenka Onwenu and attempts to figure out the best English translation of Ifemelu's Igbo name. She teases Obinze for liking only American novels. Obinze insists that America is the future.

Later, after Obinze's mother nearly catches the couple in a compromising position, she pulls Ifemelu aside. She recommends that Ifemelu and Obinze wait until university when Ifemelu has more ownership of herself before having sex. She insists that Ifemelu tell her when they start having sex so she can make sure they practice safe sex. Ifemelu feels awkward but unashamed.

ANALYSIS: CHAPTERS 3–5

Ifemelu distrusts her mother's church because it consistently keeps her mother from actively working to improve their lives. The idea that being prosperous makes one closer to God, juxtaposed with the constant passing around of the collection plate, encourages the churchgoers to give more to the church in order to demonstrate that they are prosperous and therefore godly enough to do so. Instead of providing comfort and guidance to Ifemelu's mother through their difficult financial straits, this church encourages her to ignore financial realities in order to maintain the appearance of piety. Furthermore, dismissing Ifemelu's father's difficulties as demonic keeps them from discussing their needs more honestly and perhaps from helping him to rally from his malaise. The church's advice that money is a sign of God's favor further encourages Ifemelu's mother to ignore any objections she might have to Aunty Uju's relationship with The General. These falsehoods temporarily comfort Ifemelu's mother, but they allow her to avoid working to alleviate potential damage to her family.

Obinze's delight in Ifemelu's blunt, even rude honesty contrasts with what the adults in her life want her to be, emphasizing the undercurrent of honesty in Obinze and Ifemelu's relationship. Ifemelu's father ties Ifemelu's backtalk at church to the insubordination that mars her school record, hinting that her outspoken nature will threaten her future. Aunty Uju often gives Ifemelu practical coming-of-age advice, so when she advises Ifemelu to stop speaking her mind, the implication is that growing up means suppressing one's true feelings. But Ifemelu's reputation for being difficult and argumentative makes her attractive to Obinze, even when compared with a girl like Ginika, whom the popular kids believe to be beautiful and desirable. Furthermore, Ifemelu admires Obinze for telling her exactly how he feels. Their attraction to each other's honesty despite the disapproval of those around them marks their relationship as special.

Chapter 5 continues the association of wealth and success with foreignness. The wealthy kids at school all have international visas, or, in the case of Ginika, are biracial. This ties money and prestige to the ability to leave Nigeria. Also significant is Obinze's insistence that America is the future. This statement implicitly leaves Nigeria in the past, incapable of providing opportunities. To Obinze, America is synonymous with new possibilities, an association furthered by his love of American novels. Obinze is first attracted to Ifemelu when he sees her carrying a book, and his focus on books and reading throughout *Americanah* suggests that he views what people read as both a sign of depth and a reflection of their true character. In light of this attitude, his reading of American novels means that he believes they will make him a better person in some way, either by the ideas within them or by his association with them.

Obinze's mother behaves very differently from the other Nigerian adults, representing a different vision of Nigerian adulthood that looks more like the honesty of Ifemelu and Obinze's relationship. Ifemelu compares her appearance to a famous Nigerian singer, admiring her as beautiful for looking Nigerian instead of looking partially foreign. Obinze's mother also shows an interest in Igbo, delighting in translating it as a hobby, which shows she values their heritage. Perhaps most important is her frank and unashamed willingness to discuss sex. In contrast to Ifemelu's mother, who cannot admit that her adult sister-in-law is having an affair, Obinze's mother brazenly acknowledges the truth that Ifemelu and Obinze are likely to have sex and offers practical advice and guidance for protection. Furthermore, she specifically encourages Ifemelu to take ownership of herself instead of allowing Obinze to dictate what their relationship means and the pace it takes. She encourages both Obinze and Ifemelu toward honesty in how they live and conduct themselves, as well as a lack of shame in their Nigerianness and their natural attraction.

PART 2: CHAPTERS 6–8

SUMMARY: CHAPTER 6

Aunty Uju hurries home from her job every day to wait for The General, spending money on lightening creams for her complexion. Throughout the chapter she spends money on expensive and arduous beauty regimens for The General's benefit, including shaving her pubic area because he finds the hair "disturbing."

Meanwhile, the landlord demands two years of rent from Ifemelu's family. Ifemelu knows that her father would never ask Aunty Uju for financial help, and so she decides to do so herself.

However, she learns that Aunty Uju must ask The General for the money. Aunty Uju does not receive a salary from the medical position The General invented for her. He prefers that she ask him for the things she needs. Ifemelu worries for Aunty Uju.

Aunty Uju acknowledges that she was lucky to find The General and declares that Nigeria's economy relies on kissing up to the right people. The General gifts her the money for the rent.

Ifemelu does not like The General at all when she meets him. He has coarse manners and claims Aunty Uju is different from other women because she wanted books from his trip to London. Aunty Uju becomes pregnant and insists on having the child. The General is proud of what the child indicates about his fertility and pays to have Aunty Uju deliver the baby in America. She has a son, whom she names Dike.

The General dies in a plane crash that may have been engineered by the head of state. The General's wife immediately moves to attack Aunty Uju. Friends help Aunty Uju sneak out under cover of night, and she and Dike flee to America.

SUMMARY: CHAPTER 7

Ifemelu and Obinze attend the same university in Nsukka. Because Obinze's mother moved back to Nsukka, Obinze lives in his family home, and Ifemelu lives in student housing. The university is often closed for faculty strikes because the government refuses to pay lecturers' salaries. One strike lasts long enough for students to have to go home.

During an intense make-out session in Nsukka, Obinze suggests they finally have sex. Ifemelu worries about getting pregnant, but Obinze says that if she does get pregnant, they'll just start their family. A week later Ifemelu gets a stomachache and panics. She tells Obinze and calls Aunty Uju. Obinze's mother takes Ifemelu to a doctor, who diagnoses her with appendicitis. Obinze's mother allows Ifemelu to recuperate from surgery at their house. She later confronts Ifemelu and Obinze and instructs them to use condoms. She warns Ifemelu that she cannot trust any boy to be in charge of his own protection and tells her to purchase her own condoms. Obinze sulks off.

SUMMARY: CHAPTER 8

The university lecturers now strike so often that many students leave to study abroad. Aunty Uju suggests that Ifemelu come study in America and help babysit Dike. Obinze encourages her, and his knowledge about America leads her to defer to his judgment. Ginika helps Ifemelu apply to schools. Ifemelu begins to imagine a future for herself like she's seen on American television. Ifemelu is accepted to several colleges and gets her visa on the first try. As she prepares to leave, she lets her friends come over and take what they want from her wardrobe, a bittersweet rite of passage for any friend who leaves Nigeria. Right before she leaves, Obinze's mother tells Ifemelu and Obinze to make a plan to reunite when they can.

ANALYSIS: CHAPTERS 6–8

Aunty Uju's relationship with The General demonstrates the way women are willing to demean and infantilize themselves for men in order to maintain their approval. Aunty Uju works as a doctor, yet she must ask The General for her salary as if she were a child asking for an allowance. She must in turn use some of this "allowance" money for expensive beauty treatments, like lightening creams, in order to please The General, meaning that even the money he grants her must be reinvested in keeping his interest. She also must shave her pubic region because The General is disturbed that adult women naturally grow pubic hair. This part of Aunty Uju's beauty regimen is particularly symbolic because hairlessness is a prepubescent trait, and The General requiring Aunty Uju to be hairless can also be read as a requirement to maintain the illusion of childishness. Far from being the mentor Ifemelu's mother insists he is, The General and his gifts come with the condition that Aunty Uju act like a teenager with no autonomy. While a mentor offers people opportunities to help them grow, The General wants Aunty Uju to actually regress.

Aunty Uju's story introduces the importance of women maintaining their autonomy. Aunty Uju must depend on the general entirely for financial security, which means that his death plunges her entire life into chaos. None of the measures that she believes will safeguard her position help her in the end: not the hours she spends remaking herself to his liking, not befriending his driver so that she knows what he thinks about her, not even having his child. Although Aunty Uju has a career as a doctor, because her job exists only through The General, not even her degree and education can protect her. Obinze's mother echoes this warning about the importance of independence when she tells Ifemelu she must be the one to buy condoms. While her warning against dependence on men refers to sex, this warning can metaphorically apply to protection in general. She wants Ifemelu to know that she should not expect men to have her best interests at heart in any given situation.

Although thus far Ifemelu has shown herself to be stubborn and independent, her immigration happens largely at the behest of other people, especially Obinze, revealing hidden insecurity in herself and their relationship. In Chapter 5, the class differences that allow her schoolmates to dream of the West cause Ifemelu to feel out of place and even jealous. Her decision to go to America at Obinze's behest therefore takes on a dimension of acquiescence, not entirely unlike the way Aunty Uju subverts herself for The General. Significantly, Ifemelu allows Ginika to handle the application process and help her apply to the same universities she attended. Ginika is the kind of girl other people thought Obinze would like, so attending the same schools as Ginika would allow Ifemelu to access the kind of American mystique that Ginika has developed. Despite Ifemelu's strong personality, the value placed on Ginika's attributes—her American mother, biracial looks, and now American citizenship— has led her to change the course of her life.

PART 2: CHAPTERS 9–12

SUMMARY: CHAPTER 9
There is a heat wave when Ifemelu reaches America. The heat, along with the poverty of Aunty Uju's Brooklyn neighborhood, shocks her; it is nothing like the America Ifemelu imagined from television.

Aunty Uju asks Ifemelu to move in and spend the summer baby-sitting Dike and then find a job when she goes to Philadelphia for university. Because Ifemelu needs tuition money—and her student visa does not allow her to work—Aunty Uju asks her friend Ngozi to lend Ifemelu her social security card. Ifemelu will have to pretend to be Ngozi.

Aunty Uju has grown tired and prickly over time. She uses a different accent when speaking to white Americans, allows them to mispronounce her name, and acts apologetic toward them. She will not allow Ifemelu to speak Igbo to Dike, warning that it will confuse him.

Working three jobs while caring for Dike has caused Aunty Uju to fail her medical licensing exam. Ifemelu thought Aunty Uju's American life was better than this because she never mentioned these issues in her phone calls.

SUMMARY: CHAPTER 10
Ifemelu spends her summer in Brooklyn believing that she will discover the "real America" at university. She bonds with a neighboring

Grenadian couple, Jane and Marlon, whose children play with Dike. Jane says they want to move to the suburbs because they are worried their children will start acting like black Americans. Ifemelu doesn't understand what this means.

Television commercials fascinate Ifemelu because they depict the shiny and clean America she longs to know. The news frightens her because of all the crime being reported. Aunty Uju reassures Ifemelu that America only appears more dangerous because Nigerian television does not report crime.

SUMMARY: CHAPTER 11

Aunty Uju starts dating a Nigerian immigrant named Bartholomew. Bartholomew affects American pronunciations and barely pays attention to Dike. Aunty Uju smiles demurely at him and cooks him Nigerian food. Watching television, he claims that women in Nigeria would never wear skirts as short as the women in America. Ifemelu corrects him, and he gives her a dismissive look.

Bartholomew writes comments frequently on the *Nigerian Village* website complaining about how Nigerian women go wild in America and accuses women who disagree with him of being brainwashed by the West. Ifemelu tells Aunty Uju that Bartholomew uses bleaching creams, and in Nigeria a man like him wouldn't dare speak to her. Aunty Uju counters that they are no longer in Nigeria and she wants Dike to have a sibling.

Aunty Uju finally passes her medical licensing exam. She plans to relax her hair because braids are considered unprofessional in America. Ifemelu feels that Aunty Uju has lost part of herself. Obinze, in his letters, suggests that Aunty Uju's self-effacement may be the "gratitude" of immigrant insecurity.

When Ifemelu leaves for Philadelphia, she stares at Ngozi's driver's license and social security card. She looks nothing like her, but Aunty Uju insists that to white Americans, all black people look alike.

SUMMARY: CHAPTER 12

Ginika greets Ifemelu at the bus terminal. Ginika offers advice about being American and invites Ifemelu to a party with her friends. At the party, Ifemelu wonders how all the girls know what to laugh at and understand all the cultural cues.

Ifemelu panics about spending money and even refuses to buy a winter coat. While helping Ginika shop for a dress, Ifemelu wonders if living in America will change her tastes as much as it's changed Ginika's. The cashier asks Ginika which salesgirl helped her, but

Ginika cannot remember her name. Although the salesgirls should be easy to distinguish between because one is black and one is white, the cashier asks about hair color, which does not help because both women have dark hair. Ginika explains that, in America, people pretend not to notice race.

Ifemelu moves into an apartment with other students. One of them, Elena, has a dog. Elena asks why Ifemelu won't pet her dog, and Ifemelu explains that she doesn't like dogs. Elena wants to know if it's cultural and is surprised to learn that it's just a personal preference. Ifemelu finds it odd that her roommates do not ask if someone has the money to go out before going out for food. Although she tries to socialize with her housemates, Ifemelu reels from the culture shock.

ANALYSIS: CHAPTERS 9–12

The way Ifemelu trusts the images of America on commercials and television highlights the power of media to create myths from incomplete stories. Ifemelu has associated America with wealth and success, and the media she consumed from America—along with Obinze's "expert" opinion—all supported this illusion. The uncomfortable heat wave and striking poverty that she confronts the minute she leaves the airport reveal the aspects of America that challenge her media-fueled misconceptions. Similarly, Ifemelu believed Aunty Uju was succeeding in America because of the information Aunty Uju hid in her phone calls. Aunty Uju was able to conceal the shame and stress caused by her struggle to succeed in America, thereby perpetuating the myth of America purely as a country of opportunity. Aunty Uju's observation about Nigerian news also comments on the power of images to shape one's understanding of the world. The omission of crime reports in Nigerian news creates a false sense of safety. Ifemelu is beginning to realize that incomplete stories have molded her perception of reality.

Another aspect of life in America that surprises Ifemelu is the assumed connection between black Americans and black non-Americans. Ifemelu finds Jane's insistence on keeping her children away from black American children confusing because she does not understand the stereotypes associated with black Americans. Furthermore, Ifemelu does not see why black American children in particular would influence Jane's children. Aunty Uju's behavior is more apologetic and demure in front of white Americans because she understands the implications of being a black woman under the white gaze in America. Ifemelu, however, finds this behavior mysterious and puzzling because to her, Aunty Uju is Nigerian, not a black American. In light of this confusing conflation, Aunty Uju's insistence that all black people look alike to white Americans takes on an additional meaning. Not only do white Americans conflate individual people with dark skin, they do not see the difference between black Americans and black non-Americans, even though to the people of both groups, there is a huge difference between them.

These chapters also demonstrate the conditions that immigrants face that make success in America difficult or even impossible. Despite already being a certified doctor in Nigeria, Aunty Uju must prove her medical credentials while also working menial jobs because her advanced degree will not transfer. These menial jobs keep her from studying and getting adequate sleep, which in turn prevent her from getting her medical license. Only through Ifemelu's immigration to America, which allows Aunty Uju to cut costs on babysitting, is she able to devote enough time to study and pass her test. The reality that Aunty Uju needs support from a family member emphasizes that she could not succeed without help. Ifemelu's scholarship will not cover her full college tuition, yet as an immigrant on a student visa, she cannot legally earn a salary to cover the rest, plus food and rent; she can only earn enough money by illegal means. The bureaucracy surrounding immigration means achieving the American Dream involves luck and rule bending, not just hard work.

Aunty Uju's interest in Bartholomew, despite his obvious shortcomings, reads as a kind of homesickness for old places and old patterns. His visits give her an opportunity to cook Nigerian food and talk about Nigeria. Furthermore, Bartholomew allows her to re-create a little of what she built with The General. She falls into an old habit of acting demure to impress him and dreams of having a child with him so Dike can have a sibling. However, Bartholomew lacks both the wealth and power of The General and recent knowledge of Nigeria. His judgmental comment about skirt length emphasizes that he has romanticized Nigerian life to his taste, intentionally ignoring Ifemelu, whose knowledge is current. His bleaching creams and affected accent also reveal his insecurities. Ifemelu worries at seeing Aunty Uju fall into her old pattern, because Bartholomew cannot even provide the temporary security that The General had. As Ifemelu points out, Aunty Uju has seriously lowered her standards by dating a man like Bartholomew, and the compromises she makes for the small comforts he provides expose an intense longing for her old life.

PART 2: CHAPTERS 13–16

SUMMARY: CHAPTER 13

Ifemelu applies for jobs with no success and blames herself. She has little money for groceries and cannot pay for school. When she receives junk mail, she actually feels happy because her name on the address makes her feel seen.

SUMMARY: CHAPTER 14

After Cristina Tomas, the receptionist at the registrar's office, speaks to Ifemelu as if she doesn't know English, Ifemelu practices an American accent. Obinze suggests she read American books. Ifemelu reads James Baldwin, whose work teaches her about what she calls "America's tribalisms": race, ideology, and region. She adopts American speech patterns and habits.

When discussing the film *Roots* in class, a Kenyan student, Wambui, asks why the n-word was censored and argues that censoring it erases history. The black American students in the class disagree. One black student expresses her anger at Wambui by mentioning that Africans sold the ancestors of black Americans into slavery. Wambui invites Ifemelu to a meeting of the African Students Association (ASA). At the ASA meeting, students mock the questions Americans ask them, while also mocking Africa themselves. They distinguish between American African students, who either immigrate to America young or have immigrant parents, and African American students, who are black Americans.

Aunty Uju moves to Massachusetts to marry Bartholomew. Ifemelu is shocked.

SUMMARY: CHAPTER 15

Ifemelu interviews with a tennis coach to be his personal assistant. He tells her that there are two positions, one for an office role and one for a relaxation role, and that the office position has been filled. Uncomfortable, Ifemelu asks if she can think about it.

Ginika's colleague Kimberly needs a babysitter. She would even pay Ifemelu under the table so she wouldn't have to use a fake name. Ifemelu interviews with Kimberly and Kimberly's sister, Laura. Kimberly compliments Ifemelu's name, adding that foreign cultures have wonderful names. Ifemelu realizes that Kimberly believes only people of color have cultures. The house is decorated with art from minority cultures. Kimberly shows Ifemelu a photograph of the family visiting India, commenting how happy even the poorest people were.

Kimberly's husband, Don, returns home early. Ifemelu notices that Kimberly becomes docile around him. Ifemelu doesn't get the job.

Ifemelu is a week late on rent. She calls the tennis coach in desperation. She tells him she won't have sex. He promises that he just needs her to let him touch her. Afterward, Ifemelu feels ashamed and blames herself. At home, she finds she has a phone message from Obinze. She cannot bring herself to respond and deletes both his messages and his emails. She grows listless, skips her classes, and stops calling her parents and Aunty Uju.

Ginika gets in touch with Ifemelu through one of her roommates. She is very worried about Ifemelu but has good news. The babysitter Kimberly hired left, and Kimberly wants to hire Ifemelu. The next day, Ginika drags her to Kimberly's house.

Ginika tells Ifemelu she has depression, but Ifemelu does not believe her because depression is for Americans.

SUMMARY: CHAPTER 16

Ifemelu tells herself she will reply to Obinze in a month, but when the time comes, she still feels unable. She stops reading Nigerian news because it reminds her of Obinze.

Ifemelu babysits Kimberly's children. Kimberly's daughter, Morgan, behaves for Ifemelu, which is surprising because Morgan's surliness drives Don to distraction. One day, Laura tells Ifemelu that she intends to switch from her daughter's doctor to a Nigerian doctor after reading that Nigerians are the most educated immigrant group. She compares the Nigerian doctor to a Ugandan woman she knew in graduate school, adding that the Ugandan was not like black Americans. Ifemelu suggests that when black Americans still couldn't vote, the Ugandan's father could attend Oxford. Laura is offended, and Ifemelu apologizes.

At a party Kimberly and Don throw, guests eagerly regale Ifemelu with stories of the charity work they do in Africa. Their constant talk of charity makes Ifemelu wish she could be among the givers instead of the assumed receivers.

Dike asks Aunty Uju why he doesn't have his father's last name and wonders if his father loved him. Aunty Uju refuses to tell him the truth. The move to Massachusetts has been difficult for Dike. Aunty Uju disciplines him often, threatening to send him back to Nigeria if he misbehaves. Dike is the only black student in his class, and the teacher accuses him of aggression. When Aunty Uju suggests that Dike's bad behavior stands out because of the color of his skin, the principal insists they do not see race.

ANALYSIS: CHAPTERS 13–16

These chapters further explore the complex relationship between black Americans and black non-Americans and how the assumed connection between them leads to conflict. Wambui's question about the n-word leads to extra hostility from her black American classmates. The black American student expresses her anger by bringing up a historical betrayal—African complicity in the slave trade—because Wambui's position feels like a betrayal to her. The black American students, who likely expect to have to explain the n-word to white students, now must explain how painful it is to someone they read as black and therefore as an ally. The American expectation that these two different groups have something in common also appears in Laura's anecdote about her Ugandan friend. Her praise of the Ugandan woman depends on insulting black Americans, and her sharing of this story implies that she wants Ifemelu to sign off on her racism. Ifemelu's response, while snarky, points out an important truth. Black Africans and black Americans have different histories that have offered them different opportunities.

Kimberly and Don's sympathy for and fetishization of foreign poverty create an ego-boosting narrative in which they are white saviors. They display artwork from minority cultures in their home, reflecting Kimberly's belief that people of color possess rich heritages, but in doing so, they attempt to make themselves look worldly by using those rich heritages to create a positive reflection of themselves. This unintentionally fetishizing behavior continues at the party when the guests attempt to ingratiate themselves with Ifemelu by talking about the charity work they do in Africa. Not only do they speak of Africa as a singular place with one culture, but their way of connecting with Ifemelu is to promise they are working to help Africa and therefore Ifemelu herself. This narrative sets Africa up as a damsel in distress that requires the money of generous Americans to save it from its problems. This dynamic is eerily similar to the one between Aunty Uju and The General. Just as The General loved the feeling of Aunty Uju needing money from him, these Americans take pleasure in giving charitably to Africa. Their generosity is not strictly about giving, but about how giving makes them feel better about themselves.

Ifemelu's shame that leads her to cut herself off from Obinze stems partially from a belief that she cannot achieve success in America without debasing herself. Her desperation for money has already forced her to assume another woman's legal identity, meaning that she cannot possibly live in America as her honest self.

Ifemelu understood that the coach had nefarious intentions, but when she arrives she realizes the extent to which her desperation for money and precarious immigration status have compromised her personal safety. The only paid job for which she is hired involves exploitation and assault. In addition to feeling like she betrayed Obinze as his girlfriend, this harsh reality contradicts with Obinze's naïve insistence that America is a land of the "future," of opportunity and success. Her sense of personal failure explains why reading Nigerian news reminds her of Obinze. Obinze and everyone else who loves her in Nigeria expect success from Ifemelu in this land of opportunity, and Ifemelu is not able to fulfill their narrative.

Dike finds himself caught between the two identities mentioned at the ASA student meeting: American African and African American. Aunty Uju associates Nigeria with punishment by threatening to send Dike there if he misbehaves and by scolding him in Igbo. Such negativity tells Dike that being Nigerian is not something to embrace or be proud of, but rather something scary and shameful. On the other hand, because the American construct of race does not distinguish between black Americans and black non-Americans, Dike faces terrible racial discrimination at school based on the bigoted stereotypes of black Americans as aggressive and unintelligent. Not only does he take on the burden of stereotypes he does not understand, but because Aunty Uju does not associate with black Americans, Dike also does not have an adult in his life who can help him understand what is happening and deconstruct the damaging messages for him. As a result, Dike receives only negative messages about who he is at a vulnerable age. In this light, we can read his question about his father as a search for something positive on which to build his identity.

Part 2: Chapters 17–19

Summary: Chapter 17

> *She had won, indeed, but her triumph was full of air.*
> *Her fleeting victory had left in its wake a vast, echoing*
> *space, because she had taken on, for too long, a pitch*
> *of voice and a way of being that was not hers.*
> (See QUOTATIONS, p. 66)

Ifemelu moves into her own apartment. After a telemarketer compliments Ifemelu for sounding American, she resolves to drop her

American accent. She wonders why she thinks sounding American is a triumph.

Ifemelu meets Blaine, a black American college professor, on the train to visit Aunty Uju. They flirt and exchange phone numbers. Ifemelu calls him when she gets off the train, but he never responds.

Aunty Uju complains about being black in a very white city. Her patients assume she isn't a doctor, and one even asks to switch to another doctor. Bartholomew is never home. Aunty Uju won't leave him because she wants another child. Dike has grown reserved. He tells Ifemelu that a camp counselor gave the other children sunscreen and said he didn't need any. He tells Ifemelu he wants to be "regular."

The chapter ends with a blog post Ifemelu later writes detailing the four tribalisms of America: class, ideology, region, and race. She explains that white Anglo-Saxon Protestants (WASPs) are always on top of the racial hierarchy, and black people are always at the bottom. Everyone else's position fluctuates.

SUMMARY: CHAPTER 18

Back in the salon, the braiders ask a South African customer why she has no accent. She explains she's been in America for a long time. Aisha asks Ifemelu why she has an accent, but Ifemelu ignores her. She worries she's made a mistake in her plans to go back to Nigeria.

A white woman named Kelsey arrives and asks if they can braid her hair. Kelsey makes assumptions about the shop owner's gratitude for American opportunities and asks if women can vote in her country. Kelsey disparages Nigerian author Chinua Achebe's novel *Things Fall Apart* for not teaching her the reality of modern Africa and instead praises a book called *A Bend in the River* for being an honest book about Africa. Ifemelu contends that *A Bend in the River* is more about longing for Europe than it is about Africa, which makes Kelsey uncomfortable. Kelsey is surprised to learn African braiding involves hair extensions.

Ifemelu thinks of Curt, her first American boyfriend. Curt is Kimberly's cousin who lives in Baltimore. He tells everyone he fell in love with Ifemelu at first laugh, but Ifemelu did not want to date a white man. Ifemelu did not actually notice his interest at first. When Curt asks Ifemelu on a date, she is in awe by how smitten he is with her. After they kiss, he says they have to tell Kimberly that they're dating. Ifemelu is surprised that this means they're dating, but agrees. He tells her that she is the first black woman he has ever dated. She never tells him about Obinze because she doesn't want to call him her ex. Curt is upbeat and optimistic in a way that seems distinctly American to Ifemelu.

SUMMARY: CHAPTER 19

Ifemelu meets Curt's mother, who informs her that even though their family is Republican, they supported civil rights. Ifemelu believes that she tolerates her son bringing home women of different ethnicities but assumes he will marry a white woman.

Dating Curt gives Ifemelu the money to live comfortably, boosting her grades and health. Curt asks her to leave her babysitting job, but she refuses. She does not tell her parents about Curt. As she approaches graduation, Ifemelu realizes that being a communications major with a foreign passport will make finding a job difficult. Curt gets her an interview for a public relations position at a Baltimore company that will help her get a green card. Ifemelu is grateful but deeply aware that her ASA friends struggle to find work with their student visas.

Before the interview, Ifemelu relaxes her hair because braids are not considered a professional style. The relaxer burns her scalp. Horrified, Curt argues that he likes her braids better. The company decides Ifemelu would be a great fit. She wonders if they would have thought the same if she had her natural hair.

The chapter ends with another blog post, in which Ifemelu writes that all minorities aspire toward whiteness and asks what WASPs aspire toward.

ANALYSIS: CHAPTERS 17–19

Ifemelu's decision to return to her Nigerian accent marks a turning point in her development because she places a limit on how much she is willing to change herself to achieve success. She reevaluates her efforts to sound American instead of Nigerian, challenging the belief that her ability to emulate American qualities is something she should feel proud of. By placing emphasis on the work she puts into affecting an American accent, she's able to categorize her accent as unnatural and inauthentic. If she were to embrace such a mannered quality over what she sees as her inherent self, she would be agreeing that a false, Americanized Ifemelu is better than her true self. Ever since Ifemelu moved to America, other people encouraged her to alter herself to survive, evidenced most concretely by Ngozi's social security card. By the end of this section, Ifemelu has the confidence to stand firm in her identity. She no longer wants to pretend to be someone she isn't in order to get ahead.

The struggles of Aunty Uju and Dike, read in conjunction with Ifemelu's blog posts, highlight the ways racism makes everyday life difficult to navigate. Aunty Uju is now qualified to practice medicine in two countries, yet white Americans still react with doubt and suspicion at the thought of her as a doctor. Dike's sad anecdote about sunscreen demonstrates the subtle ways stereotypes can hurt black people, as Dike could have gotten sunburned. Perhaps even sadder is the desire he expresses to be "regular," identifying whiteness as a default. Ifemelu's blog identifies the value American society places on whiteness and also introduces the idea that everyone aspires toward whiteness. The hierarchy of racial privilege that Ifemelu observes is evident in the way that Aunty Uju and Dike face incessant racist treatment and microaggressions. Their desire to be white, then, is the desire to live without the burdens of an intensely racist society.

The incident with Kelsey at the salon is another manifestation of the white savior attitude, as Kelsey loves the idea of Africa as long as she can control the narrative around it. She asks the women in the salon questions about their countries that presuppose poverty and sexism, meaning that the polite answers they give contribute to Kelsey's understanding of Africa as a place in need of help. She believes *Things Fall Apart*, which is written by a Nigerian author about Nigeria, is less honest than a book about an unspecified African country that focuses on Europe. *A Bend in the River*'s lack of specificity fits a Western vision of Africa as a singular place instead of a large continent with many different countries and cultures. Her desire to have African-style braids in her hair mirrors the way she speaks about Africa with authority. Kelsey uses the braids to metaphorically take ownership of an African aesthetic despite not truly understanding what they entail. She becomes annoyed at Ifemelu's objection because Ifemelu is challenging her right to dictate African authenticity.

The first introduction to Curt highlights his expectation to maintain control of the world around him at all times. He claims that Ifemelu did not respond to his advances at first because she didn't want to date a white man, which is a complete fabrication. Curt has made himself the author of their story. Furthermore, by insisting that Ifemelu was the one who worried about race, he positions himself as the more open-minded person willing to break the taboos of society without fear. Curt uses his privileges to make Ifemelu's life easier, but always in a way that is calculated to make him look generous. Ifemelu even resents the ease he creates for her, relative to the struggles of her ASA friends, which suggests that she feels ambivalent about the privilege available to her because she's his girlfriend. Ifemelu thinks of Curt immediately after the scene with Kelsey, both of whom exercise willful ignorance in order to invent a narrative that bolsters their sense of self. These parallels subtly reveal the controlling and self-serving aspects of Curt's sunny disposition and eagerness to help Ifemelu.

PART 2: CHAPTERS 20–22

SUMMARY: CHAPTER 20

Ifemelu moves to Baltimore for work. Now that she lives in the same city as Curt, she notices that he is always looking for things to do. She constantly needs to reassure him that she likes him.

Ifemelu's hair begins to fall out from the chemicals in the relaxer. Wambui encourages her to wear her hair natural, arguing that relaxers are unnatural. Wambui cuts Ifemelu's hair. Ifemelu hates it. Curt thinks Ifemelu's hair is brave. Ifemelu calls in sick out of embarrassment. Wambui directs Ifemelu to a website about natural black hair. Ifemelu reaches for Curt's laptop to look up the site. Curt panics when he sees her look at his laptop and tells her that the emails mean nothing. Ifemelu realizes he's cheating on her. Curt blames the other woman for continuing to email him and claims he only emailed back when she wouldn't stop. Ifemelu shouts that Curt's exes all had long, thick hair and storms out. Curt apologizes with flowers. Ifemelu forgives him because she thinks the other woman only boosted his ego.

When Ifemelu returns to work, her coworkers ask if her hair is a political statement. The natural hair website gives Ifemelu a community of women with hair like hers and a vocabulary to talk about it. She likens talking to the women on the website to giving testimony in church, as they reaffirm each other's beauty. Ifemelu finally loves her hair.

The blog post that ends the chapter discusses how Barack Obama's marriage to a dark-skinned black woman allows dark-skinned black women to see themselves as desirable.

SUMMARY: CHAPTER 21

> *"Dear Non-American Black, when you make the choice to come to America, you become black. Stop arguing. Stop saying I'm Jamaican or I'm Ghanaian.*

*America doesn't care. So what if you weren't 'black' in
your country? You're in America now."*

(See QUOTATIONS, p. 65)

Aunty Uju asks Ifemelu to talk Dike into wearing a nice shirt to
church. Aunty Uju keeps trying to make Dike tone himself down
because he already stands out. Ifemelu tells Dike he won't see any-
one he knows in church and promises to talk to Aunty Uju about not
making him wear the shirt again.

Curt is charming when he meets Aunty Uju. Ifemelu finds Curt's
performative charm exhausting. Aunty Uju is upset about an essay
Dike wrote about not knowing what he is. She blames America's
obsession with identity for his confusion and won't talk to him
about it.

Aunty Uju complains that Bartholomew expects her to make
dinner for him and wants to control her salary. He doesn't want to
spend money on Dike, nor does he care about Dike's school issues.
He blames racism for the banks not approving his business loan.
Aunty Uju blames Bartholomew for not moving to a city with more
opportunities for black people and the former heads of Nigeria for
ruining the country so she had to come to America. Infuriated by
Bartholomew's laziness around the house, Aunty Uju leaves him.

The chapter ends with a blog post in which Ifemelu informs other
black non-Americans that they are considered black in America.
She tells them to acknowledge the black American definition of racism, even if they don't understand why. She explains, that above,
all they must never speak about racism as if they are angry about it.

SUMMARY: CHAPTER 22
Ifemelu sees Kayode at the mall. Kayode says Obinze, who is now in
England, had asked Kayode to find her and tell him what she looks
like now. Kayode asks what happened between them. Ifemelu gives
him the cold shoulder and walks away. She worries what he will tell
Obinze after she gets into Curt's car. She wonders why Obinze is in
England when all he used to think about was America. Curt asks
about her mood. When she tells Curt she ran into a Nigerian friend,
Curt asks if Kayode was her ex-boyfriend. Ifemelu says no.

Ifemelu writes an email to Obinze, telling him that her silence
felt stupid to her, but she could not explain it. Obinze never replies.

Curt tells her that he booked her a massage, and Ifemelu comments on how sweet he is. Curt angrily retorts that he does not want
to be sweet, but that he wants to be the love of her life.

ANALYSIS: CHAPTERS 20–22

Ifemelu's emotional journey with her hair recalls her realization that she did not want to force her accent, farthering her growth toward an authentic self. When Wambui discusses relaxers, she describes them as trying to force hair into a shape it wasn't meant to have, emphasizing how unnatural it is for black hair to be straight. By learning to love her black hair as it is, Ifemelu learns to appreciate another aspect of her true, effortless self. However, because wearing her black hair means not giving into the white approval of straight hair, the people around her expect her choice to wear her hair naturally to have a political motive. She cannot simply like her hair as it is because black natural hair is not considered attractive by white society.

Aunty Uju's request that Ifemelu convince Dike to wear the shirt highlights the difference between Aunty Uju's and Ifemelu's philosophies on self-expression. In Nigeria, Aunty Uju's advice was often that Ifemelu should hide her true self, emphasizing the importance of appearing agreeable for the sake of getting ahead. Aunty Uju's fears about Dike's clothing are similar to the concerns around Ifemelu's behavior because Aunty Uju is attempting to keep Dike from getting into trouble. However, when presented with the same task Aunty Uju once had, Ifemelu encourages Dike to temporarily compromise instead of completely hiding his self-expression. She points out that no one important to him will see him wear the uncool shirt, which means that he will temporarily soothe Aunty Uju's anxieties without portraying a false persona to the people who matter to him. In addition, Ifemelu offers to get Aunty Uju on his side about the shirt, fighting back against the adult "wisdom" of not standing out. Whereas Aunty Uju's philosophy relies on hiding of one's self-expression for protection, Ifemelu is practical and finds a way for Dike to express his personality with minimal consequences.

Aunty Uju leaves Bartholomew because of his inability to provide her with a comfortable life by either American or Nigerian standards. Because she dated Bartholomew in part to re-create her relationship with The General, she expected Bartholomew to take care of her financially and behave as a father to Dike. Instead, Bartholomew takes ownership of Aunty Uju's money and refuses to allow her any control over it. Although The General also withheld Aunty Uju's money, she found this arrangement acceptable because he offered her luxuries and privileges. In America, Aunty Uju has created her own opportunities without Bartholomew's help, yet Bartholomew wants to reap all the benefits simply because he is her husband. Furthermore, he fails at being an American business-man because he is unwilling to acknowledge the structural racism faced by people who are considered black in America, choosing to give up rather than move to a city with more opportunities for black people. Aunty Uju decides that she cannot put herself aside for someone who gives nothing in return, demonstrating new growth and confidence.

Ifemelu is angry at Kayode for mentioning Obinze, because he reminds her that she is dissatisfied with Curt. While she associates her relationship with Obinze with honesty and truth, throughout the last few chapters, Ifemelu has associated Curt with performance. She notes he has a deep insecurity that leads him to constantly curry favor with everyone, from Aunty Uju to the woman he may have had an emotional affair with. Curt's false charm has a hunger about it that requires constant reassurance, as opposed to Obinze's honesty and sureness that allow for disagreement between them. After seeing Kayode, Ifemelu can barely pay attention to Curt because she is so distracted with thoughts of Obinze. Curt's surprising anger at the end of Chapter 22 foreshadows the end of their relationship, both because of the instability of his goodwill and the way he realizes that his "sweetness" cannot fully charm Ifemelu when compared to the specter of Obinze. While he doesn't explicitly know about Obinze, his shouting that he wants to be the love of Ifemelu's life suggests that he suspects the existence of a man like Obinze in her past.

PART 3: CHAPTERS 23–26

SUMMARY: CHAPTER 23

The novel shifts to follow Obinze's time as an illegal immigrant in London. Obinze meets with two Angolan men who are arranging an illegal green card marriage for him. They take a down payment on his marriage. When Obinze meets Cleotilde, his bride-to-be, Obinze double-checks that she wants to marry him, assuring her that they'll divorce as soon as he has his papers. She affirms that she's okay with it and needs the money. They decide to meet up separately to get to know each other better. He is attracted to her but does not want to act on it until after they are married.

He thinks back to before he left for London, when he felt like a failure because all his plans had involved America. However, he could not get an American visa due to the September 11 attacks and heightened fears about terrorism. He also has a difficult time finding a job. His mother decides to bring him on a research trip to London. She lists Obinze as her research assistant, giving him a six-month visa and a chance to move forward in his life. Obinze is shocked that his honest mother would turn to deceit.

SUMMARY: CHAPTER 24

The next few chapters describe Obinze's early London experiences. His first job in London is cleaning toilets, a humorous cliché. One day he finds feces left on the toilet seat, clearly an intentional message for the company. Humiliated, Obinze leaves it untouched and storms off. That night, he gets the email from Ifemelu. He had been hurt and furious when he realized that she had been in touch with other people and not him. Her calm tone, combined with his shame at cleaning toilets, infuriates him, and he deletes the email.

Obinze lives with his cousin Nicholas and Nicholas's wife, Ojiugo. In Nsukka, Nicholas and Ojiugo had been rebellious, glamorous college students. In London, they are models of respectability. Nicholas speaks to Ojiugo in the same tone of voice as he does his two children. Ojiugo claims that Nicholas behaves this way because he only recently got his papers and lived in constant fear before that. When Ojiugo talks to fellow mothers, they spend the time comparing their children's test scores. They gossip about a black mother who is surprised another black woman can afford to sign her children up for the youth orchestra. Obinze tells Ojiugo that his mother used to predict that Ojiugo would become a literary critic. Ojiugo explains that all her hopes are centered on her children now.

SUMMARY: CHAPTER 25

Emenike, Obinze's college friend, now lives in London with his white wife, Georgina, and seems too busy to help Obinze. Another family friend of Obinze's introduces him to a man named Vincent Obi, who will let Obinze use his National Insurance card if Obinze will give him a percentage of his salary. Obinze tries to haggle, but ultimately has no choice.

SUMMARY: CHAPTER 26

Obinze, using the name Vincent, takes a few jobs. He experiences hostility from white coworkers as well as camaraderie with fellow immigrants, who deal with white British people mangling their names. After hurting his knee at one job, his coworkers joke that he is a "knee-grow." He finds a job making deliveries for a warehouse. His cheerful boss, Roy, likes him and gives him good hours. The other warehouse workers all share elaborate, lascivious stories about women, and they assume Obinze is a ladies' man. When Obinze claims that he hasn't been having sex because he has a girlfriend in Nigeria, Roy asks if she used witchcraft on him. One of his fellow drivers, Nigel, offers to sightsee with Obinze after deliveries. Obinze likes Nigel because he splits their tips evenly, unlike the other drivers. He notices that Nigel's opinion of people often depends on how posh their accents are. Once, a Jamaican immigrant woman offers Obinze an extra tip and calls him "brother".

One day Nigel asks Obinze what to say to a girl he likes and is disappointed when Obinze tells him just to be honest with her about his feelings.

ANALYSIS: CHAPTERS 23–26

Even when approaching a sham marriage for a green card, Obinze attempts to cultivate honesty in the relationship. He double-checks Cleotilde's consent to the marriage and makes his intentions clear to her, assuring no misunderstanding. When he realizes the Angolans hold power over both of them, he organizes a meeting with Cleotilde alone so that they can speak together as themselves without being pressured to behave in a specific way. Even his desire to not act on his attraction to her until after the marriage speaks to Obinze's love of honesty. He needs Cleotilde to marry him so that he can stay in London, which makes their relationship transactional. Once they are free from that business obligation, they can get to know each other as people. Obinze's ability to cultivate honesty in an inherently dishonest situation shows how much he values truth, but also hints at an inability to survive the difficult bureaucracy of immigration that forces people into dishonest and dangerous situations.

The sad case of Nicholas and Ojiugo offers a model of immigration in which parents sacrifice their own dreams for the next generation. The extreme contrast between their rebellious youth and their dutiful and tame immigrant adulthood reveals how much immigration has forced them to change in order to survive. Ojiugo's excuse for Nicholas—that living in fear has exhausted him—shows the dire consequences of illegal immigration for the immigrant. We can infer that Nicholas had to work to be invisible, and as a result, he had to hide and conform to expectations. Their main way of relating as husband and wife now is through conversations about their children's progress, implying that their marriage has ceased to be about them connecting as individuals. Ojiugo explicitly says that all her hopes are on her children now, which means she sees no more possibilities for herself. The pressures and demands of immigration have drained Nicholas and Ojiugo of their sense of self, leaving their children to live their dreams for them.

Obinze deletes Ifemelu's email because of the shame he feels at not succeeding in his immigrant life. Because he views Ifemelu as a successful immigrant, he does not want to admit that his life in London is illegal and demeaning. Instead of finding success or "the future," Obinze cannot even let himself be noticed by other people. In his jealous viewing of the passersby, he envies them their visibility—the fact that others are allowed to see and acknowledge their existence without causing them danger. The excrement on the toilet seat highlights Obinze's invisibility as well. Obinze notices that whoever left the stool did so to send a message to the company, but he, not a high-level member of the company, receives the message. The disgruntled employee did not account for Obinze's existence in his display of anger. Like Ifemelu, Obinze must pretend to be someone else in order to work, and this vulnerability subjects him to exploitation from Vincent with no legal recourse. Just as Ifemelu's shame led her to cut off contact, Obinze's shame now causes him to delete her email.

Similar to Ifemelu's discovery of the importance placed on race, Obinze quickly realizes that white British people treat him differently or make strange assumptions about him on the basis of his being black and foreign. Some of the discrimination is overt, such as the crude knee pun his first coworkers make. Other forms are subtler, such as the drivers at the warehouse who refuse to split their tips with him. Even Roy's friendliness is charged with stereotypes. For example, he invokes the myth of African witchcraft to explain Obinze's fidelity. The assumption that Obinze has some special ability with women draws from stereotypes of black men of any origin as being hyper-sexualized. Ojiugo also notes this discrimination in the way her children are two of the few black children in prestigious activities. The Jamaican woman's extra tip also implies camaraderie among black immigrants and suggests that she may assume Obinze's white coworkers don't share tips with him.

PART 3: CHAPTERS 27–30

SUMMARY: CHAPTER 27

Obinze tries to avoid reading British newspapers because there are constant articles about needing to crack down on immigration. He sits on the train and notices the woman across from him reading a fear-mongering article about asylum seekers. He wonders if the authors of these articles realize that the immigrants come from the countries that Britain created. The woman closes the paper and looks at Obinze. Obinze wonders if she is thinking he is one of the illegal immigrants the paper warned about. Later, as he rides to Essex, which has more immigrants, he feels lonely as he compares the life he'd planned to live to its reality.

SUMMARY: CHAPTER 28

One morning, Obinze notices the men at the office avoiding his eyes and panics that he's been discovered as an illegal immigrant. Instead, they are throwing him a birthday party, or, rather, a birthday party for Vincent, whose birthday it is. The camaraderie makes Obinze feel safe.

That night, Vincent calls Obinze and demands a raise. Obinze ignores him, believing that Vincent would not be willing to risk losing all the money he gets through Obinze. However, the next day, Roy tells him someone called to report him as an illegal immigrant and asks Obinze to bring in his passport the next day.

Years later, when Chief asks Obinze to find a white man to present as his general manager, he offers Nigel the job.

SUMMARY: CHAPTER 29

> They would not understand why people like him,
> who were raised well fed and watered but mired in
> dissatisfaction, conditioned from birth to look towards
> somewhere else, eternally convinced that real lives
> happened in that somewhere else, were now resolved
> to do dangerous things . . . none of them starving . . .
> but merely hungry for choice and certainty.
>
> (See QUOTATIONS, p. 66)

The Angolans extort more money out of Obinze. Obinze is running out of money, so he goes to Emenike. Emenike tells endless stories about besting the white coworkers who underestimate them and flaunts his expensive clothes. He claims that he cannot visit Nigeria because Georgina would not survive a visit. Finally, Emenike gives Obinze the money he needs, but insists Obinze count it. Georgina calls and invites them both to dinner. Emenike warns Obinze not to tell her about the green card marriage. To Obinze's surprise, Georgina is competent and worldly, not the fragile woman Emenike portrayed her as, and much older than he is. Emenike insists on taking Obinze to a fine dining restaurant.

At Georgina's insistence, Obinze attends a party at her and Emenike's house. The party guests discuss Emenike and Georgina's trip to America. Emenike claims that Americans are friendly but do not try to pronounce foreign names correctly, while the British are suspicious of friendliness but careful with foreign names. Georgina adds that American nationalism is garish. This leads to a discussion of race in America and that Britain is not as bad. Obinze suggests that this is because the British care more about class, and Emenike gets annoyed at Obinze for stealing his point. Georgina encourages Emenike to tell his story of being snubbed by a cab driver. He tells it with humor, but Obinze remembers that when Emenike told him about the incident, he was furious. A guest comments that it's important that Britain remains a sanctuary for people fleeing war-torn countries. Obinze realizes that they would not understand someone like him, who immigrated because he believed leaving Nigeria was the key to having more choices.

SUMMARY: CHAPTER 30
It is the day of Obinze's wedding. However, at the courthouse, two policemen arrest him. The lawyer assigned to him is shocked when Obinze says that he'll willingly return to Nigeria. At the holding cell at Manchester Airport, he asks the immigration officer if he can have something to read, surprising the officer. However, his only entertainment option is to watch television after lunch. He believes that unlike the others in the cell, he is too soft, too dependent on the truth to try and immigrate again.

He thinks of Ifemelu and wonders what she would think of him now. Nicholas and Ojiugo visit him with money and new clothes. Ojiugo keeps asking Obinze if they are treating him well, which annoys Obinze because he feels that's not what's important.

Obinze and the other deportees must sit at the very back of the plane. When the immigration officer leads them back to an office to fill out paperwork, he asks for a bribe. Obinze's mother awaits him at the airport.

ANALYSIS: CHAPTERS 27–30
Both the British panic around and pity for illegal immigrants create a self-serving narrative. Obinze observes that the panicked immigration articles ignore how many immigrants come from former British colonies, meaning that Britain itself instilled the idea that

Britain has more opportunities. He describes this as an erasure of history because Britain does not acknowledge its own role in attracting immigrants. Although they appear more sympathetic, the guests at Georgina's party are also self-serving in their desire to impress Obinze with their sympathy for refugees. Their care about immigrant plight lies in the assumption that immigrants come to Britain because they need shelter, and therefore deserve British benevolence. In contrast, Obinze had a comfortable middle-class life in Nigeria, which he sacrifices for an unstable life in London, reversing his social and financial status. The guests don't consider that he might be an illegal immigrant because he does not fit into their narrative of an African who needs their pity. Both narratives allow British people to feel their country is superior to those of immigrants.

Although Emenike has achieved success in England, his success is based on superficial materiality and not personal contentment. In his boasts to Obinze, Emenike focuses on name dropping the brands he is wearing, as if to show off that he can now afford them. His tasteless insistence that Obinze count the money needlessly emphasizes the amount, belaboring the fact that Emenike is now wealthy enough to loan Obinze the money. These large gestures don't mask his clear insecurity. Emenike claims Georgina could not handle visiting Nigeria or knowing the harsh realities of immigration that Obinze faces. However, Obinze notes that Georgina appears worldly, not one to be fazed by life's difficulties. Emenike's clear lie suggests that he worries not about Georgina's sensibilities, but about how his past in Nigeria and knowing an illegal immigrant would reflect on him. His anger at Obinze for stealing attention at the party highlights his insecurities because Emenike considers Obinze's intelligence a threat to his standing among his friends. Emenike doesn't fully believe that he can trust his wife or his friends with the difficult parts of himself.

Although the guests at Emenike and Georgina's party deny that British society is racist, Obinze's experiences in London suggest otherwise. Obinze's coworkers at one of his first jobs joked at his expense explicitly about his blackness. Emenike's insistence that, unlike Americans, British people are careful to pronounce foreign names contradicts the reality of Obinze's immigrant coworkers. Emenike's own behavior around the white guests echoes Ifemelu's blog post that offers advice for non-American black people who realize that they are black in America. Just as Ifemelu instructs her readers to turn stories about their experiences with racism into funny anecdotes, Emenike erases his anger over the taxi story and makes it lighthearted. While class does play a role in Obinze's experiences, especially in Nigel's treatment of him and others whom he believes are posh, this does not erase that Obinze's blackness has led to discrimination.

Obinze gives up on legal immigration to England because he cannot handle the inherent dishonesty in the process. He describes himself as "soft" and the truth as being something that pampered his sensibilities, which implies that he sees lying in this case not as something immoral or bad, but something that competent people do to survive immigration. His time in London has taken a great emotional toll on him, and he has become so fearful that innocuous things, from his surprise birthday party to the gaze of a stranger on the train, fill him with dread. Furthermore, the rewards of immigration do not tempt Obinze. The successful immigrant men he knows—Emenike and Nicholas—have given up parts of themselves to survive immigration. Emenike's life involves performing a role for his white friends and wife, whom he does not seem to trust with his true self. Nicholas has eroded himself to the point where he can no longer connect with his wife. Obinze's values of honesty and authenticity have no place in these modes of immigration.

PART 4: CHAPTERS 31–34

SUMMARY: CHAPTER 31

Ifemelu cheats on Curt. When Ifemelu admits her transgression, Curt asks how she could do this when he was so good to her. Later, Ifemelu wonders why she sabotaged her life. She calls Curt multiple times, but eventually accepts that he won't answer.

Time flashes forward to a cocktail party after Barack Obama wins the Democratic Party's nomination. A Haitian woman claims race was never an issue in her relationship with a white man. Ifemelu argues that in America, race is everywhere, and black people in interracial relationships often don't tell their white partners what they face. This causes Ifemelu to remember the incident that led to her blog. Curt comments that *Essence* is racially skewed for only showcasing black women. Ifemelu takes him to a bookstore to demonstrate how few dark-skinned women appear in magazines. Curt claims he didn't intend the conversation to be a big deal. Ifemelu writes an email about this to Wambui, who encourages her to start a blog. In the weeks after she breaks up with Curt, Ifemelu starts her blog with a rewrite of this email as her first post. She quotes this post at the party, proclaiming that the cure for racism is real romantic love that allows for people to be uncomfortable.

The chapter ends with a blog post in which Ifemelu writes about a metaphor for race in America: her white friend doesn't know that Michelle Obama's hair is not naturally straight.

SUMMARY: CHAPTER 32
Aunty Uju joins an organization called Doctors for Africa and goes on short missions in various countries. She has started dating a Ghanaian doctor named Kweku.

Ifemelu's parents are finally able to visit her. Ifemelu thinks her parents now seem provincial. Her mother asks her if she has a "friend," meaning a boyfriend, and warns her that women wilt like flowers. The day her parents leave, Ifemelu cries, upset that she's relieved that they have gone. She resigns from work, citing personal reasons.

SUMMARY: CHAPTER 33
The success of Ifemelu's blog shocks her. People ask to support the blog, so she puts up a PayPal link. People begin to donate, including an anonymous donor who gives her a large payment once a month. She wonders if it's Curt. Soon she adds advertisements to the sidebar. However, she does not attach her name or photo to the blog, and when featured in the media, she only goes by "the blogger."

The first diversity talk that Ifemelu gives for a company in Ohio is a disaster, and she receives an email afterward that accuses her of being racist. She realizes that the point of diversity workshops is to make people feel good about themselves.

Soon Ifemelu can afford to buy her own condo and to hire an intern. Despite her success, Ifemelu sometimes pictures her readers as a mob waiting to unmask her.

Another blog post ends the chapter, this one opening the comments up as a "safe space" for black people in America who do not talk about their blackness to vent.

SUMMARY: CHAPTER 34
Ifemelu runs into Blaine at a convention for bloggers of color. Blaine remembers her and explains that he had still been in a relationship when they met. They reconnect and eventually become lovers.

Blaine eats organic food. Unlike Ifemelu, he eats tempeh even though he doesn't like it. She thinks that he will help her become a better person. Ifemelu and Blaine move in together. Blaine begins to read her blog posts before they go live. Ifemelu makes changes based on his suggestions, but resents the process because she wants to observe, not explain. Blaine urges her to take responsibility for what she posts because people use her as an academic resource.

Ifemelu's blog post that ends the chapter discusses how it is difficult to call someone racist in America because the cultural understanding of a "racist" remains stuck in the Civil Rights era.

ANALYSIS: CHAPTERS 31–34

Curt's reaction to Ifemelu's cheating reveals the true conditional boundaries of his love for her. While Ifemelu was wrong to cheat on him, he expected her to forgive his infidelity and blamed his actions on the other woman. This disparity shows that he holds himself to a different standard of conduct from Ifemelu. He asks how Ifemelu could cheat on him when he was so good to her, which suggests a transactional element to their relationship. Curt does treat Ifemelu well in the sense that he opens opportunities for her and buys her expensive things, and he assumes that these comforts will lead to her loyalty. In other words, Curt believes Ifemelu's love and faithfulness can be bought. Beyond just being hurt in the moment, Curt retracts his love completely, unwilling to return Ifemelu's calls or consider her apology. His ability to immediately drop their relationship, in conjunction with his jealous outburst at the end of Chapter 22, casts doubt on the depth of his feelings for Ifemelu and suggests that his feelings depended on her keeping him at the center of her thoughts.

These chapters discuss the origins of Ifemelu's blog, revealing that she has discovered a way to make her frankness profitable instead of alienating. Her very first blog post grows from a personal email, something that she wrote to a friend as a true expression of how she was feeling. The ability of this post to resonate with others suggests that people actually value Ifemelu's honesty. However, she worries that her blog's ability to be profitable depends on a separation between it and herself. Ifemelu creates a calculated division between the two, giving pseudonyms to the people she discusses and refusing to include a photograph of herself, even in magazine coverage. This division suggests that she worries attaching herself to the blog will limit the value people place on her words if they know who wrote them. Her fears of being a fraud, highlighted by her picturing her readers as an angry mob, show that she does not yet trust the value of her observations.

In Ifemelu's inaugural blog post, she asserts that the key to over-coming racism is romantic love that allows for complete honesty. Her thesis underscores the primary difference between her relation-ship with Curt and her relationship with Obinze, and finds Curt lacking. Curt's insistence that he hadn't meant to make a big deal over *Essence* deflects his own discomfort about approaching a racial blind spot in his thinking. He prefers to ignore the uncom-fortable truth in order to keep things light and sunny, which means that Ifemelu cannot honestly discuss race with him. Therefore, when Ifemelu writes that true romantic love that can weather dis-comfort is the key to dismantling racism, she excludes what she felt with Curt from that depth of love. As discussed, Obinze values Ifemelu's willingness to be blunt and honest even if it sacrifices kind-ness. Ifemelu knows that love that can weather brutal honesty exists because of her love for Obinze.

From the beginning of their relationship, Ifemelu finds that dating Blaine is a constant, effortful process. Blaine's philosophy on tempeh—that he will eat something he doesn't like because he knows it's good for him—encapsulates his philosophy of life. He believes that the goodness or rightness of something makes it worth the discomfort or unpleasant effort it involves, and he believes an unwillingness to undergo this effort is "laziness." This attitude, while noble, is not something that comes naturally to Ifemelu, as exemplified by her unwillingness to eat tempeh. In the more serious case of her blog, Ifemelu views the effort and rigor Blaine expects from her as dishonesty. She is neither a black American nor an aca-demic and does not want to write like one. She prefers to use her authentic voice as a Nigerian immigrant, perhaps at the expense of social justice ideals. Blaine's goodness may be admirable, but it involves trying to change who Ifemelu is as a person.

PART 4: CHAPTERS 35–38

SUMMARY: CHAPTER 35

Ifemelu goes with Blaine to visit his sister, Shan. Shan is upset about her publisher's image choice for her book cover and has been on the phone with the marketing director all morning.

After taking a call from a French admirer, she explains that she likes how European men look at her as a woman and not a black woman. Ifemelu explains that she has had more interest from white men in America than black American men. Shan waves off her objection, claiming that her being foreign must be the reason. The publisher calls to let Shan know that they have changed the cover image.

The chapter ends with a blog post in which Ifemelu explains how Barack Obama must remain the "magic black man" in the eyes of white Americans. Ifemelu defines the "magic black man" as a wise black man who never expresses anger about racism and gently helps white people with their tragic prejudices.

SUMMARY: CHAPTER 36

Ifemelu attends a birthday party for one of Blaine's friends. Blaine's ex, a white woman named Paula, is also at the party. Ifemelu can't help but notice that Paula seems more comfortable with Blaine's crowd than she is. Paula brings up a blog post of Ifemelu's about the importance of white people listening to black people when they talk about their experiences.

The conversation turns to Barack Obama, who has just announced his presidential bid. Ifemelu likes Hillary Clinton because she doesn't know anything about Obama, but she is soon drowned out by the discussion of how Obama makes people feel.

After the party, Ifemelu tries to explain to Blaine that his connection with Paula makes her jealous. She likens it to how the fried chicken he and Paula eat is battered, unlike the Nigerian fried chicken she knows. Blaine only notices the loaded invocation of fried chicken, but tells her there's no reason to be jealous. Ifemelu knows Blaine won't cheat, but she is jealous of a desire to be good that connects Blaine and Paula.

SUMMARY: CHAPTER 37

Dike is now a popular teenager. When speaking to his friends, he uses African-American Vernacular English (AAVE). When Ifemelu asks him why, he changes the subject.

Ifemelu attends one of Shan's parties. Shan complains that her editor undermined her memoir by doubting her experiences with racism. She laments that writing about race in America is impossible because white editors want "nuance," which allows people to dismiss structural issues as individual quirks. When someone suggests Ifemelu blog about this literary problem, Shan claims that Ifemelu can write about race the way she does because she isn't American and doesn't feel the consequences of the topic. Ashamed, Ifemelu wishes Shan had told her that privately.

The chapter's ending blog post discusses people who claim Obama is multiracial instead of black. Ifemelu argues that, in America, your race is decided for you.

SUMMARY: CHAPTER 38

Boubacar is a new professor from Senegal. Blaine does not like him, possibly because Ifemelu and Boubacar instantly bond over being African. Boubacar encourages Ifemelu to apply for a Princeton humanities fellowship.

Ifemelu gets a text from Blaine about Mr. White, a black security guard at the library. Ifemelu is not fond of him because he makes sexual innuendos about her and Blaine. Blaine tells her a white librarian noticed Mr. White lend a friend his car keys and assumed he was dealing drugs. The librarian's supervisor called the police.

Blaine decides to organize a protest against the university's response. Although they never discuss her attending the protest, Blaine tells Ifemelu to text him when she gets to the library. Ifemelu does not go and instead accompanies Boubacar to a colleague's going-away lunch. Blaine texts to ask where she is, excited that even Shan came. Ifemelu claims she took a nap and overslept. Ecstatic over the turnout of his protest, Blaine tells her that they gave Mr. White his dignity back.

Ifemelu admits her lie. Blaine is horrified and hurt. Blaine tells her that it's not enough for her to write her blog; she must live it. Ifemelu realizes Blaine believes she would care more if she were a black American. Blaine gives her the cold shoulder for days, and Ifemelu goes to visit Aunty Uju.

The chapter ends with a blog post talking about how poor whites still have privilege over poor non-whites.

ANALYSIS: CHAPTERS 35–38

Ifemelu is jealous of Blaine's connection with Paula because Blaine and Paula are connected by a sense of justice. Ifemelu's fried chicken metaphor further highlights the connection she cannot experience, both because of the literal difference between American and Nigerian fried chicken and because Ifemelu doesn't have the cultural background to realize she was using a loaded example. Ifemelu tries to use food as a metaphor to demonstrate that Blaine and Paula grew up eating the same kind of food, that is, absorbing the same cultural cues, and she did not. She does not realize that black people eating fried chicken is a stereotype in America, which Blaine points out but does not explain. He expects Ifemelu to already understand the history of fried chicken. Implicitly, Paula would never use fried chicken as a metaphor because, as a white American who works toward racial justice, she avoids hurting black friends with casual racism. While Blaine may not have understood it, the interaction unintentionally proves Ifemelu's point that she will never be able to participate as fully in Blaine's justice as someone like Paula.

Throughout these chapters, Shan demonstrates her jealousy of Ifemelu by using Ifemelu's foreignness as a weapon against her, devaluing her experience. Shan repeatedly mentions that Ifemelu is not American as a way to undermine Ifemelu. For example, when Ifemelu contradicts Shan's theory that American white men don't see black women as women, Shan shuts down the conversation by saying American men just exoticize Ifemelu because she's foreign. Shan's reading contradicts the way Curt tells Ifemelu she's the first black woman he's been with, which suggests he sees her as black. This disparity could have led to a conversation, but Shan acts as if Ifemelu's foreignness means her experiences are irrelevant to the conversation. Similarly, when a party guest takes the focus off of Shan by mentioning Ifemelu's blog, Shan counters that Ifemelu's blog is only successful because she's foreign. While Ifemelu herself acknowledges her privilege as a black non-American, the point of Shan's comment here was not to illuminate Ifemelu's privilege but to downplay her success by suggesting that it was false or easy. These cutting comments show that Shan feels threatened by Ifemelu's success.

Despite Shan's self-serving personality, her observation about white editors using "nuance" as an excuse to hide the structural nature of racism rings true and echoes the value the novel places on unfiltered truths. Shan's book is a memoir, and therefore the events and racism depicted are real. The editor's opinion that Shan's actual experiences lack "nuance" means that he would prefer Shan to obfuscate her experiences, coding them in language that white readers can ignore or dismiss. Throughout the novel, trying to gloss over or dismiss difficult truths inevitably leads to harm, such as when Ifemelu's family ignores her father's depression. The harm caused by unacknowledged truths extends to other characters' experiences with racism, as when Dike's school insists that they do not see race even as they stereotype Dike. Taken as a whole, we can read American racism as portrayed in this novel as an unacknowledged truth that white America papers over and dismisses. Shan's quip about nuance perfectly encapsulates the issue.

Blaine's anger at Ifemelu in Chapter 38 stems from his unwillingness to accept her as she is. He claims that her inaction invalidates her blogging because he views her blog as a means to effect change. By not protesting, Ifemelu is not working toward change. However, Ifemelu's blogging stems from a desire to explore and share her personal experiences. While Ifemelu has always been honest about the purpose of her blog, Blaine has dismissed her stated purpose as "laziness," and his surprise here shows that he thought he could change the blog's direction. However, Ifemelu cannot write the blog Blaine wants because her perspective on race inherently differs from his because she is a black non-American. In addition, Ifemelu doesn't feel a kinship with Mr. White because she is not a black American. While she can acknowledge the injustice of the situation, it does not feel personal or immediate to her. Ifemelu's absence at the protest, therefore, only surprises Blaine because he ignores who she truly is.

PART 4: CHAPTERS 39–41; PART 5: CHAPTER 42; PART 6: CHAPTER 43

SUMMARY: CHAPTER 39
At school, Dike faces racist stereotyping. His principal accuses him of hacking into the school's computer system although he is not computer savvy. Students ask Dike for marijuana, and even the church pastor uses an approximation of AAVE when speaking to him.

Finally, Blaine returns Ifemelu's calls. They tensely cook coconut rice together, realizing how divided they've become.

Ifemelu's blog post accompanying this chapter focuses on American discomfort with race and how the language surrounding race is coded.

SUMMARY: CHAPTER 40
Ifemelu now admires Blaine more than she loves him. Ifemelu reads Barack Obama's memoir, *Dreams from My Father,* and finds it inspiring. Blaine is shocked by their shared belief in Obama, which rekindles their passion. Even their friends argue less because they are caught up in Obama's spell. Ifemelu gets the Princeton fellowship, but promises Blaine not to move until after the election. When Obama wins the nomination, they finally have sex again.

They watch Obama's speech on race. Blaine finds it immoral that Obama equates black anger and white fear. Ifemelu reminds him that Obama will not get elected if he tells the truth, but Blaine is hurt.

Shan has a nervous breakdown because her book isn't selling well. Ifemelu attempts to discuss the election, hoping Obama will make conversation easy, but Shan is ignoring the election. Ifemelu recommends Obama's book. Shan counters that she wishes people would read her book.

When Barack Obama wins the election, Dike texts Ifemelu that his president is black like he is. As Ifemelu watches Obama's acceptance speech, she feels America is beautiful.

Ifemelu's accompanying blog post praises white friends who take on the burden of explaining racism to other white people, but adds that they are few and far between.

SUMMARY: CHAPTER 41

Ifemelu's flashback ends. Aisha is still working on her hair, now upset that her Igbo boyfriend has not come to talk to Ifemelu.

Aisha asks Ifemelu how she got her green card. Aisha tried to have a green card marriage when she came to America, but her fiancé extorted money from her. Ifemelu explains that her job sponsored her green card. Aisha reveals that she couldn't go back to Senegal when her father died because she didn't have a green card. She hopes that her boyfriend will marry her so she can get a green card. Her mother is sick, and she wants to go to her funeral when she dies. Ifemelu promises that she will talk to her boyfriend for her and asks where he works. She makes sure to tip Aisha well, knowing the shop owner will take most of the fee.

Aunty Uju calls in a panic to tell Ifemelu that Dike tried to commit suicide.

SUMMARY: CHAPTER 42

Obinze worries about why Ifemelu waited four days before replying to him. He tries to research Blaine. He even revives his Facebook account to look up more about him, even though he had deleted his account because he hated the cultivated stories of people's lives.

Obinze emails Ifemelu about his mother's death. Ifemelu replies a few hours later with condolences. Ifemelu explains that she is visiting Aunty Uju for a personal matter and asks for Obinze's phone number. Obinze replies, offering all his phone numbers. When Ifemelu does not reply, he writes her long emails detailing his time in London.

Ifemelu replies and tells him about Dike's suicide attempt. She gives him a link to her blog's archives and reveals that she's postponed her return. Obinze considers visiting Ifemelu and Dike, but is interrupted by Kosi telling him that his mind is wandering.

Obinze reads the archives of Ifemelu's blog and is shocked by how American the posts seem. He feels a sense of loss that he wasn't with Ifemelu while she changed so much.

SUMMARY: CHAPTER 43

"You told him what he wasn't but you didn't tell him what he was."

(See QUOTATIONS, p. 67)

Ifemelu wonders why Dike tried to commit suicide. She gets angry at Aunty Uju, accusing her of constantly telling Dike that he is not black and not telling him what it means to be Nigerian. Aunty Uju claims that Dike suffers from depression like a lot of other teenagers. Dike tells Ifemelu that she should go back to Nigeria like she planned. Ifemelu asks if he will visit her. Dike agrees.

ANALYSIS: CHAPTERS 39–43

Ifemelu, Blaine, and their friends all seem to agree on Obama as a candidate, but not on why they like Obama or what he represents. Ifemelu and Blaine both like Obama's memoir, but they never discuss what exactly they glean from his memoir. Even after having complicated conversations about Obama with their friends, Ifemelu concludes that Obama makes all her friends agree with each other. One possible reason for this contradiction appears in the many blog posts Ifemelu writes on Obama that each portray a different aspect of what he represents. Obama is a complicated symbol that people project different hopes and expectations on, and because everyone projects their own hope onto him, they all can agree on Obama as a good presidential candidate. Because Obama holds so many different expectations, he inevitably disappoints Blaine in his willingness to be pragmatic when talking about race. The real Obama can never live up to what he represents.

Shan's uninterest in the election highlights her self-centeredness. This election has particular importance because Obama may become the first black president of the United States, and the historical nature of the election demands attention. However, Shan focuses on her book sales, a personal problem, at the expense of paying any attention to an election that has the potential to open new possibilities for black people in America. Her uninterest in Obama calls into question the sincerity of her joining Blaine's protest for Mr. White and hints that she may have participated solely to stay on her brother's good side. Shan chooses to fight actively against racism when it benefits her or makes her look good to people she cares about, but she still cares more about herself than major structural changes. This self-interest explains why she uses Ifemelu's foreignness to dismiss her opinion instead of as an opportunity to deepen the discussion. She talks about her struggles with racism to win attention and sympathy for herself, not to explore, observe, or enact change.

Although Ifemelu has found Aisha annoying throughout the novel, Aisha's honesty about her struggles creates a moment of connection between them because Ifemelu sees in Aisha a life she could have lived. As in many other places in *Americanah*, sad or difficult truths here deepen relationships and allow dialogue to move forward. Without knowing the reason for Aisha's badgering, Ifemelu assumes her to be eccentric and annoying. Now that she understands Aisha's desperation, she sees that Aisha is not malicious in assuming that Igbo people know each other, but is at the end of her emotional rope and grasping for any solution. Although Ifemelu now has some class privilege in America, her early days involved similar desperation. As evidenced by the struggles of her ASA friends, Ifemelu got her green card not out of her class privilege, or her birth, or her education, but because she was dating Curt. Because Ifemelu can now relate to Aisha, she wants to help her.

Dike's suicide attempt demonstrates how much damage the baggage of being both an American African and African American has done to him. Aunty Uju's unwillingness to tell him the truth about his father or give him any positive associations with his Nigerian roots has cut Dike off from a sense of pride in his Nigerianness. At the same time, white Americans insist on treating Dike as a black American, projecting onto him cultural baggage that he does not know how to navigate and that Aunty Uju insists doesn't belong to him. Even though Aunty Uju tells him that he is not black, he is still stereotyped, as evidenced by his consistently bad treatment by the school administration and his classmates assuming that he is a drug dealer. While Ifemelu lashes out in anger and admonishes Aunty Uju for never telling Dike "what he was," she makes a reasonable point. If Dike is neither black nor Nigerian, his identity is a double negative. He is not truly a black American, but he does not feel Nigerian because he does not know what that means.

PART 7: CHAPTERS 44–47

SUMMARY: CHAPTER 44

Ifemelu's friend Ranyinudo greets her at the airport in Lagos. At first, Lagos overwhelms Ifemelu, and she cannot figure out whether the country has changed or she has. Ranyinudo calls her "Americanah," a teasing term for Nigerians who come back from America with American affectations.

In Ranyinudo's flat, NTA (Nigerian Television Authority) plays a patriotic fluff story, which Ranyinudo mocks. Ranyinudo never watches NTA and, in fact, rarely watches any Nigerian stations at all. Ranyinudo's salary from her advertising job does not cover her rent, and she is dating a wealthy married man. She complains that her lover was supposed to get her a new car. The electricity has been off for a week, and Ranyinudo must run her loud generator until she goes to bed.

SUMMARY: CHAPTER 45

Ifemelu has a job lined up as a features editor at *Zoe*, a women's magazine. The owner of the magazine, Aunty Onenu, loves the idea of having an editor who lived in America and insists that Ifemelu visit her at home. Ifemelu finds this request unprofessional, but reminds herself that in Nigeria boundaries are blurred. She dreams of transforming *Zoe* into a great magazine and shares her ideas with Aunty Onenu. Aunty Onenu is more interested in proving that *Zoe* is better than its competitor, *Glass*. Ranyinudo warns Ifemelu that if she hadn't just come from America, Aunty Onenu would have fired her for coming in with constructive criticism.

In searching for a flat of her own, Ifemelu discovers being an Americanah opens doors. A landlord who only rents to expats is willing to make an exception for a returnee from America, even though she is Igbo. She pays two years of rent in advance and then realizes that people take bribes because most people cannot afford to pay this much at once. When Ifemelu yells at tile workers for doing a subpar job and threatens not to pay them, Ranyinudo tells her she's finally acting like a Nigerian.

Ranyinudo asks why Ifemelu did not call Obinze to ask him for help on getting a nice flat. Ifemelu realizes that for Ranyinudo, men function as objects to manipulate. She has not yet told Obinze that she's back in Nigeria, although she replies to his emails.

SUMMARY: CHAPTER 46

Ifemelu visits her parents on the weekends. She lies to her parents and friends that she and Blaine are still together. Her friends talk about marriage often, and the lie protects her from her married friends' pity and from being expected to join in single friends' jealousy.

Her friend Priye is now a wedding planner. A recent client had seven governors attend her wedding. Ifemelu asks why governors are the sign of a successful wedding. Her friends explain that they show the couple is well connected. Priye and Ranyinudo declare that the rule in Lagos is to marry the man who can best maintain you.

SUMMARY: CHAPTER 47

Aunty Onenu brags that most of *Zoe*'s staff are graduates of foreign universities. There are only three editors on staff, and aside from Ifemelu, only Doris graduated from an American university. Doris tries to ally herself with Ifemelu over their shared Americanah-ness. Ifemelu resents Doris's assumption that they see the world the same way, so when Zemaye comments on Doris leaving the air conditioning too cold, Ifemelu takes Zemaye's side. However, Doris and Ifemelu later bond over finding quirks in Nigerian dialect jarring. Doris invites Ifemelu to a meeting of the Nigerpolitan Club, a club for Nigerians returning from abroad.

ANALYSIS: CHAPTERS 44–47

Ranyinudo's affair echoes Aunty Uju's relationship with The General, showcasing that reliance on wealthy men is a survival mechanism for Nigerian women who lack opportunities. Ranyinudo has a respectable job, yet still cannot afford her rent, signifying a discrepancy between the cost of living and wages in Lagos. Ranyinudo and Priye's declaration that marriage is about finding a man to "maintain them" implies that women cope with being underpaid by relying on wealthy men to make their lives easier. This calls back to how Aunty Uju could not find a job without The General creating one for her, which allowed him to further control her life. Because of Aunty Uju's fall from grace, the comparison between them makes clear that Ranyinudo's life is fragile and dependent on her boyfriend's continued success and favor. The inability to get by on an honest wage also echoes Ifemelu's early American experiences, in which she couldn't pay rent or education without working illegally. These similarities highlight that, without money and opportunity, women turn to demeaning and dangerous activities and relationships just to get by.

Despite returning from America in order to embrace her true Nigerian self, Ifemelu finds that many aspects of her new life in Lagos value superficiality over truth. Ranyinudo refuses to watch Nigerian television stations because they largely show propaganda, highlighting that the government's official policy is to hide difficult truths from the public. Just as Ifemelu's outspokenness got her into trouble as a child, her frank suggestions to Aunty Onenu nearly jeopardize her position because Aunty Onenu expects unconditional respect as the head of the magazine. In addition, Aunty Onenu focuses on the prestige her foreign-educated editors bring her instead of putting any value on content or taking Ifemelu's suggestions into consideration. Priye's job as a wedding planner seems to be less about celebrating the couples' love and more about making couples appear prestigious. Priye's services allow couples to pay for their reputation, reducing their wedding to a display of influence. Ifemelu has become more authentic in her time away, but Lagos has remained committed to its preference for pretenses.

Ranyinudo frequently calls Ifemelu an Americanah, but others value Ifemelu's returnee status more than she does. Aunty Onenu forgives Ifemelu's outspokenness because she associates it with an American attitude, even though Ifemelu has always been this blunt. This aspect of Ifemelu hasn't changed, but her returnee status changes how Nigerians perceive her personality. Ifemelu's landlord rents to Ifemelu because he believes her return from America makes her reliable. The value Nigerians place on her returnee status, therefore, is another way Nigerians put a greater value on foreignness. In addition, Doris's assumption that she and Ifemelu see the world in the same way because they both attended university in America suggests that she expects Ifemelu to join her in reveling in this newfound Americanah status. Doris pointedly runs the air conditioning high as if to highlight that she lived in a colder climate for a while, and expects Ifemelu to do the same. She is surprised when Ifemelu rejects her camaraderie, because it means Ifemelu doesn't embrace being an Americanah. The label of Americanah is something others project onto Ifemelu, not something she cultivates.

PART 7: CHAPTERS 48–51

SUMMARY: CHAPTER 48

The Nigerpolitan Club members complain about the things they miss from abroad. Ifemelu recognizes that even she has self-righteousness in her voice and hates it. Fred, a Harvard graduate, invites her to get a drink. She declines, but tells him to call her.

Summary: Chapter 49

Ifemelu hates working at *Zoe*. During an editorial meeting, Aunty Onenu criticizes Ifemelu's interview for being judgmental. Ifemelu argues that this is no way to beat *Glass*. Doris argues their content is just like *Glass*'s. Aunty Onenu leaves the editorial meeting to go shopping, and Ifemelu uses a call from Ranyinudo as an excuse to take a break.

Ranyinudo's lover is withholding a Jeep he bought for her because she's not acting like the "sweet girl" she used to be. Ifemelu thinks the phrase "sweet girl" means that Ranyinudo lets him dictate who she is.

Doris asks the secretary, Esther, how she's feeling. Ifemelu is ashamed she didn't notice Esther was sick. Ifemelu asks Esther what medicine she's taking. Esther brings her an unlabeled bottle. Ifemelu, shocked a doctor would give out unlabeled medication, suggests they run a health column. Doris counters that they are not activists. Ifemelu begins to envision a blog about Lagos.

Ifemelu complains about the articles *Zoe* runs. Doris explains that the women featured pay Aunty Onenu and that is the way things work in Nigeria. Ifemelu says that she can never tell what Doris's true opinions are. Doris calls Ifemelu judgmental and asks why she wants to make Aunty Onenu's magazine about her. Ifemelu warns Doris that following Aunty Onenu will not lead to success. On the way out of the office, Esther tells Ifemelu that she has a husband-repelling spirit.

Summary: Chapter 50

Dike visits Ifemelu in Lagos. He has never seen so many black people in the same place before.

Ifemelu starts her new blog. She interviews Priye, has Zemaye write a gossip piece and writes her own op-ed about the Nigerpolitan Club. After Ifemelu posts about young women in Lagos who rely on men for their lifestyles, Ranyinudo calls her up, furious. Ifemelu insists that the post was more about Aunty Uju. Ranyinudo asks how these arrangements differ from Ifemelu's relationship with Curt. Ifemelu apologizes. Ranyinudo tells her to call Obinze because Ifemelu's emotional frustration is making her lash out.

Dike asks Ifemelu about his father. She takes him to see Aunty Uju's estate. Dike asks if he can drive them back to Ifemelu's. When he leaves, he concludes that he likes Lagos. Ifemelu is tempted to tell him to move there, but stops herself. Ranyinudo asks how a boy like Dike could want to commit suicide, calling it foreign behavior. Ifemelu is furious.

SUMMARY: CHAPTER 51

After Ifemelu mistakes a man at a bank for Obinze, she decides to text him. He calls her back immediately and asks when he can see her. She suggests they see each other immediately. They meet at the Jazzhole bookshop.

When Obinze asks her what book she came to buy, she tells him she decided that if their reunion is one to remember, she wants it to be at a place worth remembering. He is delighted by her honesty. They discuss how strange returning to Nigeria has been. Obinze flirts openly. He asks about Ifemelu's life in America, noting that he could tell she'd changed a lot after reading her blog. He no longer dreams of America because it lost its allure when he realized his wealth opened the door for him in Nigeria.

They meet again the next day. Obinze says he's pleased to talk with someone smart. Ifemelu realizes the comment is about Kosi and wonders why he married her. Obinze praises Ifemelu's blog and tells her she needs investors. Ifemelu rejects his money. He asks why Ifemelu cut off contact. Ifemelu tells him about the tennis coach and how afterward she felt like she had betrayed both herself and Obinze. Obinze acknowledges that she must have felt pain and loneliness and wishes she'd told him. Ifemelu almost cries, and as Obinze holds her hand, she feels safe.

ANALYSIS: CHAPTERS 48–51

Ranyinudo insists that Ifemelu's blog post about transactional relationships is born out of Ifemelu's emotional frustration, which brings some of Ifemelu's fears about seeing Obinze to light. She knows that Obinze is now wealthy and married, and if they were to start a relationship again, they would be in danger of falling into the same dynamic shared between Aunty Uju and The General. Because she knows that in this mode of relationship the mistress never truly gets the man's heart, she fears that she will reunite with Obinze, never truly to have him, and live with him gaining power over her emotionally and financially. Ifemelu fears the power dynamics that so easily manifest in financially unbalanced relationships, which is likely the reason she refused to ask Obinze for help in finding a flat. This fear also explains why she rejects his money in Chapter 51, keeping her blog separate from Obinze's money and dependent only on her own ambition. Her complete unwillingness to create any sort of dependence on Obinze demonstrates that Ifemelu does not believe a transactional relationship can ever be true or honest.

By quitting her job at *Zoe* to start a new blog, Ifemelu makes another move toward authenticity. While in America, Ifemelu cultivated ways to be her true self despite the pressures of American life by maintaining her true accent, refusing to relax her hair, and keeping her blog focused on her own observations surrounding race. Now, instead of accepting Doris's insistence that magazines like *Zoe* simply represent how Nigeria works, she decides to forge her own vision of journalism in Lagos that satisfies her creatively and financially. This attitude is different from that of an Americanah like Doris, because Doris, while she may not believe in *Zoe,* accepts it as the true Nigerian way. Doris believes her only recourse is to fawn over Aunty Onenu at work while complaining at the Nigerpolitan Club. Ifemelu, on the other hand, does not accept that "Nigerian" has to mean subpar, and she innovates.

Dike finds his visit to Nigeria healing because it allows him to witness and experience the truth about where he came from. Dike finds comfort in seeing black people everywhere because he grew up in the very white suburbs in Massachusetts and has never seen a place where black people are the norm. Throughout the novel, other people have told him who he is, projecting stereotypes and baggage onto him. Now Dike knows exactly who he is and where he comes from, and he can decide his own identity. Despite this affirming visit, Ifemelu does not invite Dike to move to Nigeria because she recognizes that he grew up in America. Nigeria is an important part of his identity, but not his whole identity.

The climax of the novel comes when Obinze comforts Ifemelu in the bookstore because it reaffirms the love they had as teenagers, a love that is founded on and deepens with honesty and truth. Ifemelu feels safe when Obinze reacts to her story about the tennis coach, echoing the sense of ease she felt not long after their first meeting. Even when Ifemelu tells a story about one of the lowest points of her life, Obinze creates ease in Ifemelu, allowing her to accept how she feels at that moment and be without fear of judgment. This ease and acceptance survives intercontinental distance and long silences, indicating that their love for each other has survived all of these hardships as well.

PART 7: CHAPTERS 52–55

SUMMARY: CHAPTER 52

Obinze teases Ifemelu for checking her blog on her phone over lunch. After a disappointing meal at an Italian restaurant, Ifemelu buys fried plantains from a market seller, who encourages her to get akara as well. Ifemelu admires that the woman is selling exactly what she makes, not a name brand or location.

When Obinze drops Ifemelu off, she tells him she's tired of ignoring their attraction and upset that Obinze kisses her and then goes home to his wife. Obinze asks if she's still with Blaine, and she points out that Obinze is married. Ifemelu brings up Zemaye's article on how to tell if a man is cheating. Obinze insists this doesn't feel like cheating. Ifemelu points out that no man thinks cheating feels like cheating. Obinze storms out of her flat, but returns a few minutes later, apologizing. He doesn't like to talk about their relationship as if it's just sex. Ifemelu agrees. They sleep together and, for the first time, Ifemelu understands the phrase "making love."

SUMMARY: CHAPTER 53

Ifemelu is so in love she feels like a cliché. However, the reality that Obinze is married looms. Obinze offers to cook for Ifemelu, commenting that Kosi doesn't like the idea of him cooking. He makes excuses for his marriage, explaining how vulnerable he had felt at that point in his life. Furious, Ifemelu says she plans to interview the wealthy man he dislikes. Obinze protests that she said she wasn't going to do that. They eat dinner, and Obinze reminds her that they love each other. He invites her to come with him on his trip to Abuja. Later, Obinze texts that he should go to Abuja alone because he needs to think things through. Ifemelu texts back that he's a coward.

When she returns from the salon, Obinze is parked in front of Ifemelu's flat. He tells her he needs time to think. Ifemelu is furious that he resorts to using empty words and tells him to go to hell.

SUMMARY: CHAPTER 54

In Abuja, Obinze thinks of Ifemelu. He realizes he's afraid of disrupting his life with Kosi, even though he doesn't even like his life with her very much. He calls Ifemelu multiple times, but she does not answer.

Back in Lagos, Obinze prepares to go out to dinner with Kosi for Nigel's birthday. When he sees Buchi, he remembers how Kosi apologized for having a daughter. He had been disoriented from being newly rich when he started dating Kosi and liked her predictability. That night, Kosi tries to initiate sex, but Obinze refuses. The next day, he tells Kosi he wants a divorce. Kosi argues his family is his responsibility. She reveals that she knows he's seeing Ifemelu, and he's humiliated that she knew all along.

Kosi insists he attend their friend's christening party the next day, laying out matching blue outfits for the whole family. Obinze feels like a coward for playing along with the charade. Bored and annoyed by the party, he confides in his friend that he wants to divorce Kosi and marry Ifemelu. His friend chastises him that getting divorced is white person behavior.

Summary: Chapter 55

Ifemelu watches as the male peacock that lives near her flat performs his mating dance. The female rejects him, and he looks ridiculous. Ifemelu wants to tell Obinze about it. She mourns losing Obinze. She doesn't doubt his love but believes his sense of duty keeps him from following his heart. Ranyinudo encourages her to date, but instead, Ifemelu throws herself into her blog.

Obinze appears at the door of Ifemelu's flat. He has written her a letter explaining that he does not want their separation to shadow their lives. He will divorce Kosi but continue to help raise Buchi. He echoes the words he said at Kayode's party all those years ago: "I'm chasing you." Ifemelu invites him in.

Analysis: Chapters 52–55

Ifemelu's praise of the plantain seller reflects her desire to be with Obinze without pretenses. Ifemelu admires that the woman sells exactly what she makes without pretense, which contrasts with the Italian restaurant she and Obinze came from that makes money by selling the *idea* of Italy. When they return to her flat, Ifemelu propositions Obinze directly, asking for what she wants without trying to disguise her desire as being anything but desire, similar to how the plantain seller does not try to embellish what her plantains are. Her satisfaction with simple plantains and dislike of false but fancy Italian food hints at trouble to come in her relationship with Obinze. As things stand, even if they act on their honest desires, they cannot be together honestly if Obinze is married to Kosi. If Obinze is a married man, no matter what language they may use to excuse their relationship, it will be an affair.

Kosi's response to Obinze's cheating emphasizes the difference between her and Ifemelu and the ways she embodies the superficiality of Lagos. Kosi values appearances and consistency over turbulent honesty, which recalls Aunty Onenu's foolish preference for Doris's obsequiousness over Ifemelu's constructive criticism. Kosi, like Aunty Onenu, would rather pull herself deeper into a fantasy of success, dressing her family alike, than speak honestly with Obinze about his feelings and desires. The value Kosi places on the appearance of success and happiness sets up as a foil for Ifemelu because Ifemelu's entire selfhood is based on brutal but productive honesty. The association of Kosi with pretense and Ifemelu with truth means that Obinze's choice between Kosi and Ifemelu is also a choice about how he wants to live. He can pick comfort with Kosi, who fits into Lagos society, or his honest feelings with Ifemelu.

Although Ifemelu would prefer Obinze in her life, the life she has created for herself is independent of Obinze's love, which shows that she has truly grown into herself. The self she created in America involved embracing her Nigerianness, first by reclaiming her accent and then her hair. This self-love shows that she has found a way to appreciate herself without Obinze's approval. She has built a new opportunity for herself and her friends through her blog, which she has kept independent from the influence of financial backers. Her friendship with Ranyinudo can handle difficult conversations, such as the one about the blog post, meaning that she has real friends she can count on and be honest with. Finally, she has chosen heartbreak over a dishonest life with Obinze, meaning that she values herself and her independence over romance. Though she feels sad, she doesn't regret this decision and makes no attempt to apologize or make amends for what she believes is the right decision for her life. Ifemelu's willingness to set the terms for their relationship proves that she sees herself as a complete person without Obinze.

Obinze's decision to leave Kosi for Ifemelu marks the triumph of an authentic life over one of superficial ease. Notably, Obinze moves out of the house he shares with Kosi and begins the divorce process independently of whether Ifemelu accepts his advances or not. Ifemelu has spurred Obinze to change the superficiality in his life, and he has decided this change in and of itself will be a reward, regardless of his romantic success with Ifemelu. When Obinze considers the effect of his divorce on Buchi, he decides that she eventually will realize her parents do not love each other, which he considers worse than divorce because she will feel her life has not been real. Obinze trusts in honesty's power to create the kind of life that he longs for. Ifemelu, as a representative of honesty and truth, invites Obinze into her flat because she can fully trust in Obinze's desire to build an honest life together.

Important Quotations Explained

1. She rested her head against his and felt, for the first time,
    what she would often feel with him: a self-affection. He
    made her like herself. With him, she was at ease; her skin
    felt as though it was her right size.

This quotation appears in chapter 4, during Obinze and Ifemelu's
initial flirtation. This feeling of contentment that Ifemelu has with
Obinze sets up the feeling Ifemelu misses throughout her time as an
immigrant in America. The word "ease" has particular importance
because it highlights how with Obinze, Ifemelu does not need to make
an effort to change herself. Especially early on in her immigration,
Ifemelu believes she must change herself to succeed, often leading
to self-doubt and insecurity. Because of her student visa, she must
literally pretend to be someone else in order to work, and when she
fails to get a job, she blames herself. Cristina Tomas's condescension
leads her to change her accent. Blaine makes her believe she needs
to be a better person, causing her to change her eating habits and
her blogging style. This ease—and her loss of it—emphasizes why
Obinze is so important to Ifemelu and the high stakes resting on
their reunion.

2. "Dear Non-American Black, when you make the choice to
    come to America, you become black. Stop arguing. Stop
    saying I'm Jamaican or I'm Ghanaian. America doesn't
    care. So what if you weren't 'black' in your country?
    You're in America now."

This quotation, which comes from the blog post that ends Chapter
21, sums up Ifemelu's realization that Americans do not differentiate between black Americans and black non-Americans. A major
part of the post details the ways this conflation means that black
non-Americans need to accept and work within the rules of this
identification in order to cope with the racist structures in America.
Despite Aunty Uju's insistence that Dike is not black, Dike cannot

escape the racism and microaggressions that black Americans must deal with. While Ifemelu is at university, the black Americans in her class become angry at Wambui's disagreement with them over the use of the n-word in fiction. They are angry in part because they did not expect to have to explain the pain of the n-word to a person who looks black, and because the white people listening could use Wambui's reasoning to justify their own use of the word. In all these cases, attempting to ignore or go against expectations for black Americans makes life more complicated and difficult for black non-Americans.

3.   She had won, indeed, but her triumph was full of air. Her fleeting victory had left in its wake a vast, echoing space, because she had taken on, for too long, a pitch of voice and a way of being that was not hers.

This quotation from the beginning of Chapter 17 marks the moment Ifemelu decides to stop faking an American accent after a telemarketer compliments her by telling her she sounds American. Ifemelu initially adopts an American accent because Cristina Tomas, the university registrar's receptionist, speaks to her as if she does not understand English well, causing Ifemelu to feel ashamed of her own accent. However, Ifemelu is not American, and by allowing herself to accept sounding American as an achievement, she accepts that being American is something to aspire to over being Nigerian. In this quotation, she acknowledges that American mannerisms and speech are not hers naturally, emphasizing that she still sees herself as Nigerian at heart. The telemarketer's comment therefore constitutes an empty victory because she does not value Americanness over Nigerianness, nor does she see herself as an American. This pivotal realization marks her first step to reclaiming her identity as a Nigerian woman and embracing her authentic self.

4.   They would not understand why people like him, who were raised well fed and watered but mired in dissatisfaction, conditioned from birth to look towards somewhere else, eternally convinced that real lives happened in that somewhere else, were now resolved to do dangerous things . . . none of them starving . . . but merely hungry for choice and certainty.

Obinze makes this observation at Georgina and Emenike's dinner party in Chapter 29. As the dinner guests passionately talk about the importance of Britain remaining open to refugees, Obinze realizes that their image of an African illegal immigrant is someone fleeing desperate circumstances, someone who requires their benevolence. As the son of a university professor, Obinze had not been desperate until he immigrated to London, where his status as an illegal immigrant is taking an emotional toll on him and making it extremely difficult to earn money. He has scrubbed toilets and committed fraud based on a seemingly false promise of a better life. The contradiction between what white British people imagine illegal African immigrants and Obinze's reality demonstrates how the image of a war-torn Africa allows the party guests to feel good about themselves as saviors. In light of this, Obinze believes that the people at the dinner party would not react well to his story because his suffering does not allow them to be heroes, but instead makes them complicit in the myth that the West is the only land of opportunity.

5.   "You told him what he wasn't but you didn't tell him what he was."

Ifemelu makes this comment to Aunty Uju in Chapter 43, when she blames Aunty Uju for causing Dike's suicide attempt. While the blame may not lie entirely on Aunty Uju, Ifemelu's observation has merit. Aunty Uju emotionally damages Dike by hiding the truth about his roots, echoing the value the novel places on authenticity and honesty. Aunty Uju's refusal to tell Dike the truth about her relationship with The General leads Dike to assume that his father did not love him, making him feel unwanted. Although the truth is not pretty, Dike gains confidence from learning about The General. Throughout Dike's life in America, Aunty Uju has not allowed him to learn about being Nigerian other than by threatening to send him back to Nigeria as punishment and scolding him in Igbo. Therefore, Dike has negative associations with his Nigerian heritage. Because Dike finds himself caught between a heritage cloaked in lies and the negative experiences that come with being mistaken for a black American, Dike cannot build an authentic sense of self.

Key Facts

FULL TITLE
Americanah

AUTHOR
Chimamanda Ngozi Adichie

TYPE OF WORK
Novel

GENRE
Sociopolitical fiction

LANGUAGE
English

TIME AND PLACE WRITTEN
2011–2012; Cambridge, Massachusetts

DATE OF FIRST PUBLICATION
May 2013

PUBLISHER
Alfred A. Knopf

NARRATOR
An anonymous third-person narrator

POINT OF VIEW
The narrator speaks in the third person and follows Ifemelu
for most of the chapters, but sometimes follows Obinze.
The narrator offers no insight, allowing Ifemelu or Obinze's
thoughts and feelings to comment on the events around them.
Some of the chapters include Ifemelu's blog posts, which she
writes in first person, and are subjective, based on her own
observations of and opinions on race in America.

TONE
Ifemelu and Obinze's observations of other characters'
hypocrisies and blind spots often lend the novel a satirical
tone. Ifemelu's blog posts are witty and funny but also bitingly
satirical.

TENSE
Past tense

SETTING (TIME)
The present time that frames the novel is around 2009. Ifemelu's flashback sections begin in the early 1990s, and Obinze's London section takes place around 2002, not long after the September 11 attacks.

SETTING (PLACE)
Lagos and Nssuka, Nigeria; various cities on the East Coast of the United States; and London, England.

PROTAGONISTS
Ifemelu and Obinze

MAJOR CONFLICT
After Ifemelu leaves her childhood sweetheart, Obinze, in Nigeria to immigrate to America, she must navigate the difficulties of immigrant life in order to forge her own identity.

RISING ACTION
Ifemelu leaves Nigeria to study in America and cuts off contact with Obinze after being sexually assaulted; in America, Ifemelu experiences what it's like to be labeled as "black" for the first time and grapples with her identity.

CLIMAX
Back in Nigeria, Ifemelu tells Obinze the truth of why she cut off contact, and Obinze reacts with care and acceptance; it becomes clear that the honesty and sense of ease that has underpinned their love from the beginning has survived their long separation.

FALLING ACTION
Ifemelu and Obinze carry on an affair, but Ifemelu gets angry at Obinze for not being honest with his feelings and staying with Kosi. Obinze leaves Kosi and tells Ifemelu that he wants to be with her.

THEMES
The importance of authenticity; race and racism

MOTIFS
Reading and novels; lies

SYMBOLS
Barack Obama; hair; the male peacock

KEY FACTS

STUDY QUESTIONS

1. *How does Ifemelu's relationship with Obinze differ from her relationships with Curt and Blaine?*

Unlike Ifemelu's other boyfriends, Obinze does not attempt to change Ifemelu or her priorities. Curt is happy to make Ifemelu's life easy and luxurious as long as she allows him to control the narrative of their relationship. For example, when talking about their courtship, Curt fabricates a story about Ifemelu not wanting to date a white man, rewriting their story to paint him as an open-minded white man who won over a distrusting black woman. Blaine attempts to improve Ifemelu by discouraging what he perceives as her "laziness." What he views as her putting insufficient effort into dismantling racist assumptions in her blog, Ifemelu sees as trying to write as her authentic Nigerian self who does not have an innate understanding of American racial issues. In contrast with Curt and Blaine, Obinze accepts Ifemelu just as she is, making it easier for her to do likewise. She does not need to alter her priorities for Obinze, nor must she allow him to dictate her reality. This ease and honesty, above all, distinguishes their relationship.

2. *What is the importance of Ifemelu's blog?*

Ifemelu's blog allows her to profit and live by the same outspokenness that got her into trouble as a girl. Ifemelu grew up with the message that her desire to be honest was a detriment to her life. In the incident at church, Ifemelu is punished for telling the truth and admonished by Aunty Uju that she does not always have to say her every thought. The other students assume Obinze would want a nice girl like Ginika, whereas Ifemelu's argumentative nature makes her too much of an effort to date. However, by blogging, Ifemelu monetizes her expression of uncomfortable truths and feelings. Commenters consider her insights important and thought-provoking, enough for advertisers to find her site profitable and for her to be invited to conferences and gain media coverage. Ifemelu's ability to make a living from blogging proves that she can live as her true self, outspoken and prickly, and others will value her insights and truth telling. At the end, her decision to create a new Lagos blog highlights her growing into her authentic self because she trusts that she can profit from her honesty in the country where she feels the most herself.

3. *The novel's title, Americanah, is a term for a Nigerian who has returned from America with American affectations. At the end of the novel, has Ifemelu truly become an Americanah? Why or why not?*

While living in America has changed Ifemelu, she does not truly embody the idea of an Americanah because she doesn't base her identity on being a returnee from America. Ifemelu's growth throughout the novel has been toward embracing her authentic self, highlighted by her embracing her Nigerian accent and natural hair, and then finally returning to Nigeria. While she does find comfort at the Nigerpolitan Club, she also finds their rejection of Nigeria to be performative. For example, when Ifemelu and Fred talk, she notes the number of unnecessary references they use in conversation to make themselves seem more impressive and educated. She notes in her blog post on the Nigerpolitan Club that attempting to change Lagos is futile because Lagos will always be its eclectic self, which sounds similar to Ifemelu's own journey. All attempts to change or improve Ifemelu—such as Aunty Uju's warnings not to speak her mind or Blaine's organic food—ultimately fail. She describes Lagos as being "assorted," full of many different aspects, just as Ifemelu has been shaped by her Nigerian identity as well as her American experiences. Instead of an Americanah who borrows a persona, Ifemelu is herself, as multifaceted as the city she loves.

How to Write Literary Analysis

The Literary Essay: A Step-by-Step Guide

When you read for pleasure, your only goal is enjoyment. You might find yourself reading to get caught up in an exciting story, to learn about an interesting time or place, or just to pass time. Maybe you're looking for inspiration, guidance, or a reflection of your own life. There are as many different, valid ways of reading a book as there are books in the world.

When you read a work of literature in an English class, however, you're being asked to read in a special way: you're being asked to perform *literary analysis*. To analyze something means to break it down into smaller parts and then examine how those parts work, both individually and together. Literary analysis involves examining all the parts of a novel, play, short story, or poem—elements such as character, setting, tone, and imagery—and thinking about how the author uses those elements to create certain effects.

A literary essay isn't a book review: you're not being asked whether or not you liked a book or whether you'd recommend it to another reader. A literary essay also isn't like the kind of book report you wrote when you were younger, when your teacher wanted you to summarize the book's action. A high school or college–level literary essay asks, "How does this piece of literature actually work?" "How does it do what it does?" and, "Why might the author have made the choices he or she did?"

The Seven Steps

No one is born knowing how to analyze literature; it's a skill and a process you can master. As you gain more practice with this kind of thinking and writing, you'll be able to craft a method that works best for you. But until then, here are seven basic steps to writing a well-constructed literary essay:

1. *Ask questions*
2. *Collect evidence*
3. *Construct a thesis*

1. Ask Questions

When you're assigned a literary essay in class, your teacher will often provide you with a list of writing prompts. Lucky you! Now all you have to do is choose one. Do yourself a favor and pick a topic that interests you. You'll have a much better (not to mention easier) time if you start off with something you enjoy thinking about. If you are asked to come up with a topic by yourself, though, you might start to feel a little panicked. Maybe you have too many ideas—or none at all. Don't worry. Take a deep breath and start by asking yourself these questions:

- **What struck you?** Did a particular image, line, or scene linger in your mind for a long time? If it fascinated you, chances are you can draw on it to write a fascinating essay.

- **What confused you?** Maybe you were surprised to see a character act in a certain way, or maybe you didn't understand why the book ended the way it did. Confusing moments in a work of literature are like a loose thread in a sweater: if you pull on it, you can unravel the entire thing. Ask yourself why the author chose to write about that character or scene the way he or she did, and you might tap into some important insights about the work as a whole.

- **Did you notice any patterns?** Is there a phrase that the main character uses constantly or an image that repeats throughout the book? If you can figure out how that pattern weaves through the work and what the significance of that pattern is, you've almost got your entire essay mapped out.

- **Did you notice any contradictions or ironies?** Great works of literature are complex; great literary essays recognize and explain those complexities. Maybe the title of the work seems to contradict its content (for example, the play *Happy Days* shows its two characters buried up to their waists in dirt). Maybe the main character acts one way around his or her family and a completely different way around his or her friends and associates. If you can find a way to explain a work's contradictory elements, you've got the seeds of a great essay.

At this point, you don't need to know exactly what you're going to say about your topic; you just need a place to begin your exploration. You can help direct your reading and brainstorming by formulating your topic as a *question*, which you'll then try to answer in your essay. The best questions invite critical debates and discussions, not just a rehashing of the summary. Remember, you're looking for something you can *prove or argue* based on evidence you find in the text. Finally, remember to keep the scope of your question in mind: is this a topic you can adequately address within the word or page limit you've been given? Conversely, is this a topic big enough to fill the required length?

GOOD QUESTIONS

"Are Romeo and Juliet's parents responsible for the deaths of their children?"

"Why do pigs keep showing up in Lord of the Flies?*"*

"Are Dr. Frankenstein and his monster alike? How?"

BAD QUESTIONS

"What happens to Scout in To Kill a Mockingbird?*"*

"What do the other characters in Julius Caesar *think about Caesar?"*

"How does Hester Prynne in The Scarlet Letter *remind me of my sister?"*

---

2. COLLECT EVIDENCE

Once you know what question you want to answer, it's time to scour the book for things that will help you answer the question. Don't worry if you don't know what you want to say yet—right now you're just collecting ideas and material and letting it all percolate. Keep track of passages, symbols, images, or scenes that deal with your topic. Eventually, you'll start making connections between these examples, and your thesis will emerge.

Here's a brief summary of the various parts that compose each and every work of literature. These are the elements that you will analyze in your essay and that you will offer as evidence to support your arguments. For more on the parts of literary works, see the Glossary of Literary Terms at the end of this section.

Elements of Story   These are the *what*s of the work—what happens, where it happens, and to whom it happens.

- **Plot:** All the events and actions of the work.

- **Character:** The people who act and are acted on in a literary work. The main character of a work is known as the *protagonist*.

- **Conflict:** The central tension in the work. In most cases, the protagonist wants something, while opposing forces (antagonists) hinder the protagonist's progress.

- **Setting:** When and where the work takes place. Elements of setting include location, time period, time of day, weather, social atmosphere, and economic conditions.

- **Narrator:** The person telling the story. The narrator may straightforwardly report what happens, convey the subjective opinions and perceptions of one or more characters, or provide commentary and opinion in his or her own voice.

- **Themes:** The main idea or message of the work—usually an abstract idea about people, society, or life in general. A work may have many themes, which may be in tension with one another.

Elements of Style   These are the *how*s—how the characters speak, how the story is constructed, and how language is used throughout the work.

- **Structure and organization:** How the parts of the work are assembled. Some novels are narrated in a linear, chronological fashion, while others skip around in time. Some plays follow a traditional three- or five-act structure, while others are a series of loosely connected scenes. Some authors deliberately leave gaps in their work, leaving readers to puzzle out the missing information. A work's structure and organization can tell you a lot about the kind of message it wants to convey.

- **Point of view:** The perspective from which a story is told. In *first-person point of view*, the narrator involves himself or herself in the story. ("I went to the store"; "We watched in horror as the bird slammed into the window.") A first-person narrator is usually the protagonist of the work, but not always. In *third-person point of view*, the narrator does not participate in the story. A third-person narrator may closely follow a specific character, recounting that individual character's thoughts or experiences, or it may be what we call an *omniscient* narrator. Omniscient narrators see and know all: they can witness any event in any time or place and are privy to the inner thoughts and feelings of all characters. Remember that the narrator and the author are not the same thing!

- **Diction:** Word choice. Whether a character uses dry, clinical language or flowery prose with lots of exclamation points can tell you a lot about his or her attitude and personality.

- **Syntax:** Word order and sentence construction. Syntax is a crucial part of establishing an author's narrative voice. Ernest Hemingway, for example, is known for writing in very short, straightforward sentences, while James Joyce characteristically wrote in long, extremely complicated lines.

- **Tone:** The mood or feeling of the text. Diction and syntax often contribute to the tone of a work. A novel written in short, clipped sentences that use small, simple words might feel brusque, cold, or matter-of-fact.

- **Imagery:** Language that appeals to the senses, representing things that can be seen, smelled, heard, tasted, or touched.

- **Figurative language:** Language that is not meant to be interpreted literally. The most common types of figurative language are *metaphors* and *similes*, which compare two unlike things in order to suggest a similarity between them— for example, "All the world's a stage," or "The moon is like a ball of green cheese." (Metaphors say one thing *is* another thing; similes claim that one thing is *like* another thing.)

---

3. CONSTRUCT A THESIS

When you've examined all the evidence you've collected and know how you want to answer the question, it's time to write your thesis statement. A *thesis* is a claim about a work of literature that needs to be supported by evidence and arguments. The thesis statement is the heart of the literary essay, and the bulk of your paper will be spent trying to prove this claim. A good thesis will be:

- **Arguable.** "*The Great Gatsby* describes New York society in the 1920s" isn't a thesis—it's a fact.

- **Provable through textual evidence.** "*Hamlet* is a confusing but ultimately very well-written play" is a weak thesis because it offers the writer's personal opinion about the book. Yes, it's arguable, but it's not a claim that can be proved or supported with examples taken from the play itself.

- **Surprising.** "Both George and Lenny change a great deal in *Of Mice and Men*" is a weak thesis because it's obvious. A really strong thesis will argue for a reading of the text that is not immediately apparent.

- **Specific.** "Dr. Frankenstein's monster tells us a lot about the human condition" is *almost* a really great thesis statement, but it's still too vague. What does the writer mean by "a lot"? *How* does the monster tell us so much about the human condition?

GOOD THESIS STATEMENTS

Question: In *Romeo and Juliet*, which is more powerful in shaping the lovers' story: fate or foolishness?

Thesis: "Though Shakespeare defines Romeo and Juliet as 'star-crossed lovers,' and images of stars and planets appear throughout the play, a closer examination of that celestial imagery reveals that the stars are merely witnesses to the characters' foolish activities and not the causes themselves."

Question: How does the bell jar function as a symbol in Sylvia Plath's *The Bell Jar*?

Thesis: "A bell jar is a bell-shaped glass that has three basic uses: to hold a specimen for observation, to contain gases, and to maintain a vacuum. The bell jar appears in each of these capacities in *The Bell Jar*, Plath's semi-autobiographical novel, and each appearance marks a different stage in Esther's mental breakdown."

Question: Would Piggy in *The Lord of the Flies* make a good island leader if he were given the chance?

Thesis: "Though the intelligent, rational, and innovative Piggy has the mental characteristics of a good leader, he ultimately lacks the social skills necessary to be an effective one. Golding emphasizes this point by giving Piggy a foil in the charismatic Jack, whose magnetic personality allows him to capture and wield power effectively, if not always wisely."

LITERARY ANALYSIS

4. DEVELOP AND ORGANIZE ARGUMENTS

The reasons and examples that support your thesis will form the middle paragraphs of your essay. Since you can't really write your thesis statement until you know how you'll structure your argument, you'll probably end up working on steps 3 and 4 at the same time. There's no single method of argumentation that will work in every context. One essay prompt might ask you to compare and contrast two characters, while another asks you to trace an image through a given work of literature. These questions require different kinds of answers and therefore different kinds of arguments. Below, we'll discuss three common kinds of essay prompts and some strategies for constructing a solid, well-argued case.

TYPES OF LITERARY ESSAYS

- **Compare and contrast**

  Compare and contrast the characters of Huck and Jim in The Adventures of Huckleberry Finn.

  Chances are you've written this kind of essay before. In an academic literary context, you'll organize your arguments the same way you would in any other class. You can either go *subject by subject* or *point by point*. In the former, you'll discuss one character first and then the second. In the latter, you'll choose several traits (attitude toward life, social status, images and metaphors associated with the character) and devote a paragraph to each. You may want to use a mix of these two approaches—for example, you may want to spend a paragraph apiece broadly sketching Huck's and Jim's personalities before transitioning to a paragraph or two describing a few key points of comparison. This can be a highly effective strategy if you want to make a counterintuitive argument—that, despite seeming to be totally different, the two characters or objects being compared are actually similar in a very important way (or vice versa). Remember that your essay should reveal something fresh or unexpected about the text, so think beyond the obvious parallels and differences.

- **Trace**

  Choose an image—for example, birds, knives, or eyes—and trace that image throughout Macbeth.

  Sounds pretty easy, right? All you need to do is read the play, underline every appearance of a knife in *Macbeth* and then list them in your essay in the order they appear, right? Well, not exactly. Your teacher doesn't want a simple catalog of examples. He or she wants to see you make *connections* between those examples—that's the difference between summarizing and analyzing. In the *Macbeth* example, think about the different contexts in which knives appear in the play and to what effect. In *Macbeth*, there are real knives and imagined knives; knives that kill and knives that simply threaten. Categorize and classify your examples to give them some order. Finally, always keep the overall effect in mind. After you choose and analyze your examples, you should come to some greater understanding about the work, as well as the role of your chosen image, symbol, or phrase in developing the major themes and stylistic strategies of that work.

- **Debate**

  Is the society depicted in 1984 *good for its citizens?*

  In this kind of essay, you're being asked to debate a moral, ethical, or aesthetic issue regarding the work. You might be asked to judge a character or group of characters *(Is Caesar responsible for his own demise?)* or the work itself *(Is* Jane Eyre *a feminist novel?)*. For this kind of essay, there are two important points to keep in mind. First, don't simply base your arguments on your personal feelings and reactions. Every literary essay expects you to read and analyze the work, so search for evidence in the text. What do characters in *1984* have to say about the government of Oceania? What images does Orwell use that might give you a hint about his attitude toward the government? As in any debate, you also need to make sure that you define all the necessary terms before you begin to argue your case. What does it mean to be a "good" society? What makes a novel "feminist"? You should define your terms right up front, in the first paragraph after your introduction.

Second, remember that strong literary essays make contrary and surprising arguments. Try to think outside the box. In the *1984* example above, it seems like the obvious answer would be no, the totalitarian society depicted in Orwell's novel is *not* good for its citizens. But can you think of any arguments for the opposite side? Even if your final assertion is that the novel depicts a cruel, repressive, and therefore harmful society, acknowledging and responding to the counterargument will strengthen your overall case.

---

5. WRITE THE INTRODUCTION

Your introduction sets up the entire essay. It's where you present your topic and articulate the particular issues and questions you'll be addressing. It's also where you, as the writer, introduce yourself to your readers. A persuasive literary essay immediately establishes its writer as a knowledgeable, authoritative figure.

An introduction can vary in length depending on the overall length of the essay, but in a traditional five-paragraph essay it should be no longer than one paragraph. However long it is, your introduction needs to:

- **Provide any necessary context.** Your introduction should situate the reader and let him or her know what to expect. What book are you discussing? Which characters? What topic will you be addressing?

- **Answer the "So what?" question.** Why is this topic important, and why is your particular position on the topic noteworthy? Ideally, your introduction should pique the reader's interest by suggesting how your argument is surprising or otherwise counterintuitive. Literary essays make unexpected connections and reveal less-than-obvious truths.

- **Present your thesis.** This usually happens at or very near the end of your introduction.

- **Indicate the shape of the essay to come.** Your reader should finish reading your introduction with a good sense of the scope of your essay as well as the path you'll take toward proving your thesis. You don't need to spell out every step, but you do need to suggest the organizational pattern you'll be using.

Your introduction should not:

- **Be vague.** Beware of the two killer words in literary analysis: *interesting* and *important*. Of course, the work, question, or example is interesting and important—that's why you're writing about it!

- **Open with any grandiose assertions.** Many student readers think that beginning their essays with a flamboyant statement, such as "Since the dawn of time, writers have been fascinated by the topic of free will," makes them sound important and commanding. In fact, it sounds pretty amateurish.

- **Wildly praise the work.** Another typical mistake student writers make is extolling the work or author. Your teacher doesn't need to be told that "Shakespeare is perhaps the greatest writer in the English language." You can mention a work's reputation in passing—by referring to *The Adventures of Huckleberry Finn* as "Mark Twain's enduring classic," for example—but don't make a point of bringing it up unless that reputation is key to your argument.

- **Go off-topic.** Keep your introduction streamlined and to the point. Don't feel the need to throw in all kinds of bells and whistles in order to impress your reader—just get to the point as quickly as you can, without skimping on any of the required steps.

---

6. WRITE THE BODY PARAGRAPHS

Once you've written your introduction, you'll take the arguments you developed in step 4 and turn them into your body paragraphs. The organization of this middle section of your essay will largely be determined by the argumentative strategy you use, but no matter how you arrange your thoughts, your body paragraphs need to do the following:

- **Begin with a strong topic sentence.** Topic sentences are like signs on a highway: they tell the readers where they are and where they're going. A good topic sentence not only alerts readers to what issue will be discussed in the following paragraphs but also gives them a sense of what argument will be made *about* that issue. "Rumor and gossip play an important role in *The Crucible*" isn't a strong topic sentence because it doesn't tell us very much. "The community's constant gossiping creates an environment that allows false accusations to flourish" is a much stronger topic sentence—

it not only tells us what the paragraph will discuss (gossip) but how the paragraph will discuss the topic (by showing how gossip creates a set of conditions that leads to the play's climactic action).

- **Fully and completely develop a single thought.** Don't skip around in your paragraph or try to stuff in too much material. Body paragraphs are like bricks: each individual one needs to be strong and sturdy or the entire structure will collapse. Make sure you have really proven your point before moving on to the next one.

- **Use transitions effectively.** Good literary essay writers know that each paragraph must be clearly and strongly linked to the material around it. Think of each paragraph as a response to the one that precedes it. Use transition words and phrases such as *however*, *similarly*, *on the contrary*, *therefore*, and *furthermore* to indicate what kind of response you're making.

---

7. WRITE THE CONCLUSION

Just as you used the introduction to ground your readers in the topic before providing your thesis, you'll use the conclusion to quickly summarize the specifics learned thus far and then hint at the broader implications of your topic. A good conclusion will:

- **Do more than simply restate the thesis.** If your thesis argued that *The Catcher in the Rye* can be read as a Christian allegory, don't simply end your essay by saying, "And that is why *The Catcher in the Rye* can be read as a Christian allegory." If you've constructed your arguments well, this kind of statement will just be redundant.

- **Synthesize the arguments rather than summarizing them.** Similarly, don't repeat the details of your body paragraphs in your conclusion. The readers have already read your essay, and chances are it's not so long that they've forgotten all your points by now.

- **Revisit the "So what?" question.** In your introduction, you made a case for why your topic and position are important. You should close your essay with the same sort of gesture. What do your readers know now that they didn't know before? How will that knowledge help them better appreciate or understand the work overall?

- **Move from the specific to the general.** Your essay has most likely treated a very specific element of the work—a single character, a small set of images, or a particular passage. In your conclusion, try to show how this narrow discussion has wider implications for the work overall. If your essay on *To Kill a Mockingbird* focused on the character of Boo Radley, for example, you might want to include a bit in the conclusion about how he fits into the novel's larger message about childhood, innocence, or family life.

- **Stay relevant.** Your conclusion should suggest new directions of thought, but it shouldn't be treated as an opportunity to pad your essay with all the extra, interesting ideas you came up with during your brainstorming sessions but couldn't fit into the essay proper. Don't attempt to stuff in unrelated queries or too many abstract thoughts.

- **Avoid making overblown closing statements.** A conclusion should open up your highly specific, focused discussion, but it should do so without drawing a sweeping lesson about life or human nature. Making such observations may be part of the point of reading, but it's almost always a mistake in essays, where these observations tend to sound overly dramatic or simply silly.

A+ ESSAY CHECKLIST

Congratulations! If you've followed all the steps we've outlined, you should have a solid literary essay to show for all your efforts. What if you've got your sights set on an A+? To write the kind of superlative essay that will be rewarded with a perfect grade, keep the following rubric in mind. These are the qualities that teachers expect to see in a truly A+ essay. How does yours stack up?

- ✓ Demonstrates a thorough understanding of the book
- Presents an original, compelling argument
- Thoughtfully analyzes the text's formal elements
- Uses appropriate and insightful examples
- Structures ideas in a logical and progressive order
- Demonstrates a mastery of sentence construction, transitions, grammar, spelling, and word choice

LITERARY ANALYSIS

Suggested Essay Topics

1. Compare and contrast Ifemelu and Obinze's struggles in finding work. What factors account for their different experiences?

2. Throughout the novel Ifemelu and Obinze attend several distinctly uncomfortable parties. What makes these parties awkward and why?

3. Obinze observes that the writers of the fearmongering articles about immigrants must find comfort in their denial of history. What other characters in the novel rely on their denials of history, and how do these denials help or hurt them?

4. Ifemelu decides to return to Nigeria because she feels that she has "cement in her soul." What is weighing her down?

5. What role does mental health and depression play in the novel? Is depression really an "American disease"?

GLOSSARY OF LITERARY TERMS

ANTAGONIST

The entity that acts to frustrate the goals of the *protagonist*. The antagonist is usually another *character* but may also be a nonhuman force.

ANTIHERO / ANTIHEROINE

A *protagonist* who is not admirable or who challenges notions of what should be considered admirable.

CHARACTER

A person, animal, or any other thing with a personality that appears in a *narrative*.

CLIMAX

The moment of greatest intensity in a text or the major turning point in the *plot*.

CONFLICT

The central struggle that moves the *plot* forward. The conflict can be the *protagonist*'s struggle against fate, nature, society, or another person.

FIRST-PERSON POINT OF VIEW

A literary style in which the *narrator* tells the story from his or her own *point of view* and refers to himself or herself as "I." The narrator may be an active participant in the story or just an observer.

HERO / HEROINE

The principal *character* in a literary work or *narrative*.

IMAGERY

Language that brings to mind sense-impressions, representing things that can be seen, smelled, heard, tasted, or touched.

MOTIF

A recurring idea, structure, contrast, or device that develops or informs the major *themes* of a work of literature.

NARRATIVE

A story.

LITERARY ANALYSIS

NARRATOR

The person (sometimes a *character*) who tells a story; the *voice* assumed by the writer. The narrator and the author of the work of literature are not the same thing.

PLOT

The arrangement of the events in a story, including the sequence in which they are told, the relative emphasis they are given, and the causal connections between events.

POINT OF VIEW

The *perspective* that a *narrative* takes toward the events it describes.

PROTAGONIST

The main *character* around whom the story revolves.

SETTING

The location of a *narrative* in time and space. Setting creates mood or atmosphere.

SUBPLOT

A secondary *plot* that is of less importance to the overall story but that may serve as a point of contrast or comparison to the main plot.

SYMBOL

An object, *character*, figure, or color that is used to represent an abstract idea or concept.

SYNTAX

The way the words in a piece of writing are put together to form lines, phrases, or clauses; the basic structure of a piece of writing.

THEME

A fundamental and universal idea explored in a literary work.

TONE

The author's attitude toward the subject or *characters* of a story or poem or toward the reader.

VOICE

An author's individual way of using language to reflect his or her own personality and attitudes. An author communicates voice through *tone*, *diction*, and *syntax*.

A Note on Plagiarism

Plagiarism—presenting someone else's work as your own—rears its ugly head in many forms. Many students know that copying text without citing it is unacceptable. But some don't realize that even if you're not quoting directly, but instead are paraphrasing or summarizing, it is plagiarism unless you cite the source.

Here are the most common forms of plagiarism:

- Using an author's phrases, sentences, or paragraphs without citing the source
- Paraphrasing an author's ideas without citing the source
- Passing off another student's work as your own

How do you steer clear of plagiarism? You should always acknowledge all words and ideas that aren't your own by using quotation marks around verbatim text or citations like footnotes and endnotes to note another writer's ideas. For more information on how to give credit when credit is due, ask your teacher for guidance or visit www.sparknotes.com.

LITERARY ANALYSIS

Review & Resources

Quiz

1. Why does Ifemelu have to go to Trenton to get her hair braided?

    A. Her favorite salon is in Trenton
    B. She wants to try out a new salon
    C. The salon in Princeton closed
    D. There are no African hair braiding salons in Princeton

2. Who does Kayode originally want to set Obinze up with?

    A. Ranyinudo
    B. Priye
    C. Ifemelu
    D. Ginika

3. What does Obinze say made him notice Ifemelu?

    A. She was carrying a novel
    B. Her braided hair
    C. Her fashionable clothing
    D. She was singing

4. Why must Aunty Uju wait to give Ifemelu's family money?

    A. Hospital workers are on strike
    B. She must ask The General for money
    C. Her next paycheck comes in a week
    D. Ifemelu's father won't take it at first

5. What does Obinze's mother tell Ifemelu after she catches them fooling around?

    A. Ifemelu should tell her when they start having sex
    B. Ifemelu should break up with Obinze
    C. Ifemelu and Obinze should get married
    D. Ifemelu and Obinze should not have sex before marriage

6. Why does Ifemelu need to use someone else's ID card to get a job?

    A. She lost hers
    B. People aren't hiring immigrants
    C. Her student visa won't allow her to work
    D. She hates the photo on her card

7. Which author does Ifemelu read at the library?

    A. Toni Morrison
    B. J. K. Rowling
    C. Chinua Achebe
    D. James Baldwin

8. What must Ifemelu do before her job interview?

    A. Buy a suit
    B. Relax her hair
    C. Get a work visa
    D. Create a fake work history

9. Who encourages Ifemelu to wear her hair natural?

    A. Wambui
    B. Obinze
    C. Aunty Uju
    D. Curt

10. Why is Dike upset about the camp counselor not giving him sunscreen?

    A. He's afraid of getting a sunburn
    B. The other campers laughed at him
    C. He got in trouble with Aunty Uju
    D. He wants to be normal

11. What does Aunty Uju blame for Dike's essay?

    A. America's focus on identity
    B. His school
    C. Bartholomew
    D. Dike being mad at her

12.   What does Nigel assume about Obinze?

    A.   That he's an illegal immigrant
    B.   That he hates British food
    C.   That he's good with women
    D.   That he's from America

13.   What does Obinze ask the detention officers for?

    A.   A lawyer
    B.   A book
    C.   Internet access
    D.   A better seat on the plane

14.   According to Curt, which magazine has racial bias?

    A.   Vogue
    B.   Essence
    C.   Wired
    D.   Tiger Beat

15.   In regard to her blog posts, what does Blaine accuse
      Ifemelu of?

    A.   Not truly caring about race
    B.   Not really understanding her posts
    C.   Laziness
    D.   Plagiarism

16.   What is Shan upset about when Ifemelu first meets her?

    A.   A breakup with a boyfriend
    B.   Her haircut
    C.   A friend's betrayal
    D.   Her book's cover

17.   What draws Blaine and Ifemelu back together?

    A.   Barack Obama
    B.   Coconut rice
    C.   John Coltrane
    D.   Nigeria

18. What does Aisha ask Ifemelu as she finishes braiding her hair?

    A. To go to her boyfriend's work
    B. How Ifemelu got her papers
    C. How much braids cost in Nigeria
    D. For her social security card

19. What delays Ifemelu's return to Nigeria?

    A. Visa problems
    B. Obinze's marriage
    C. Dike's suicide attempt
    D. A fight with Blaine

20. What is Aunty Onenu's goal for *Zoe*?

    A. To teach Nigerian women about feminism
    B. To win an award for journalism
    C. To gain American distribution
    D. To sell more copies than *Glass*

21. What is the Nigerpolitan Club?

    A. A bar
    B. A meetup for returning Nigerians
    C. A bookstore
    D. A dating website

22. Where do Ifemelu and Obinze reunite?

    A. A bookstore
    B. A jazz club
    C. A party
    D. A market

23. When Obinze decides not to bring Ifemelu to Abuja, what does she accuse him of?

    A. Cowardice
    B. Having another lover
    C. Not loving her enough
    D. Leading her on

24.   Why does Kosi tell Obinze he should stay?

    A.   She loves him

    B.   Ifemelu will leave him

    C.   He has a responsibility to his family

    D.   He's going through a midlife crisis

25.   What does Obinze tell Ifemelu after he reads her his letter?

    A.   I love you

    B.   Yori Yori

    C.   Run away with me

    D.   I'm chasing you

ANSWER KEY

1. D; 2. D; 3. A; 4. B; 5. A; 6. C; 7. D; 8. B; 9. A; 10. D; 11. A; 12. C; 13. B; 14. B; 15. C; 16. D; 17. A; 18. B; 19. C; 20. D; 21. B; 22. A; 23. A; 24. C; 25. D

Suggestions for Further Reading

Achebe, Chinua. *Things Fall Apart*. New York: Anchor, 1994.

Adichie, Chimamanda Ngozi. "'Americanah' Author Explains 'Learning' To Be Black in the US." By Terry Gross. *Fresh Air on NPR*. June 27, 2013. https://www.npr.org/templates/transcript/transcript.php?storyId=195598496.

Adichie, Chimamanda Ngozi. "The Danger of a Single Story." TEDGlobal 2009, July 2009. http://www.ted.com/talks/chimamanda_adichie_the_danger_of_a_single_story/transcript.

Adichie, Chimamanda Ngozi. *We Should All Be Feminists*. New York: Anchor, 2015.

Emenyonu, Ernest N., ed. *A Companion to Chimamanda Ngozi Adichie*. Woodbridge, Suffolk, UK: James Currey, 2017.

Hagher, Iyorwuese. *Nigeria: After the Nightmare*. Lanham, Maryland: University Press of America, Inc., 2011.

Obama, Barack. *Dreams from My Father: A Story of Race and Inheritance*. New York: Broadway Books, 2004.

Reddy, Emily. "Take Note: Noted Nigerian Author Chimamanda Ngozi Adichie Talks about Her Novel 'Americanah.'" WPSU, November 14, 2014. https://radio.wpsu.org/post/take-note-noted-nigerian-author-chimamanda-ngozi-adichie-talks-about-her-novel-americanah.

REVIEW & RESOURCES

NOTES

NOTES

NOTES

NOTES

Notes

Notes

Notes

NOTES

NOTES

Notes

Notes

NOTES

NOTES